SONNY'S GIRLS

At Hazelhurst High, Meredith, Cyndi and Jennifer had been football hero Sonny's girls. Now, ten years later, none could forget the night that changed their lives forever.

"I've never forgotten touching you. I remember every stroke of my flesh against yours, the taste of your mouth against mine...."

With a groan, Ryder kissed Jennifer.

At the touch of his lips, Jennifer pulled away a fraction, gazing up at him in shock for a moment before drawing his mouth back to hers. How could one man's kiss be different from all the others? she wondered dizzily, lifting her hands to his hair, curling her fingers in its soft thickness. How could its effect be so much more shattering? And how could she have forgotten this heat? This bliss?

She pressed herself against him, a wellspring of memories pouring over her. Not unpleasant memories this time, not oppressive, but just as real and maybe more poignant.

In that moment, Jennifer realized that no other man's kiss had ever affected her, that no other man had ever touched her. She had pretended there wasn't a hollow place inside, a door unopened.

But now that the door had been reopened, what was she to do?

Dear Reader,

Welcome to Silhouette **Special Edition** . . . welcome to romance. Each month, Silhouette **Special Edition** publishes six novels with you in mind—stories of love and life, tales that you can identify with—romance with that little "something special" added in.

This month, Silhouette **Special Edition** has some wonderful stories in store for you, including the finale of the poignant series SONNY'S GIRLS, *Longer Than . . .* by Erica Spindler. I hope you enjoy this tender tale! *Annie in the Morning* by Curtiss Ann Matlock is also waiting for you in September. This warm, gentle, emotional story is chock-full of characters that you may well be seeing in future books. . . .

Rounding out September are winning tales by more of your favorite writers: Jo Ann Algermissen, Christine Flynn, Lisa Jackson and Jennifer Mikels! A good time will be had by all!

In each Silhouette **Special Edition** novel, we're dedicated to bringing you the romances that you dream about—the type of stories that delight as well as bring a tear to the eye. And that's what Silhouette **Special Edition** is all about—special books by special authors for special readers!

I hope you enjoy this book and all of the stories to come.

Sincerely,

Tara Gavin
Senior Editor

ERICA SPINDLER
Longer Than...

Silhouette Special Edition

Published by Silhouette Books New York

America's Publisher of Contemporary Romance

For Celeste Hamilton and Emilie Richards
Whew—we did it!
(And we're still friends)
I love you guys
You're the greatest

SILHOUETTE BOOKS
300 East 42nd St., New York, N.Y. 10017

LONGER THAN...

ISBN: 0-373-09696-8

First Silhouette Books printing September 1991

Printed in the U.S.A.

ERICA SPINDLER

came to writing from the visual arts and has numerous one-person, invitational and group exhibitions to her credit. She still teaches art classes in addition to her writing. "It seems only natural to me that I should be writing romance," says Erica. "My paintings had the same spirit of optimism and romanticism that my stories do."

A descendant of Marie Duplessis, who was the most famous courtesan of her day and the inspiration for Dumas's work *Camille,* Erica lives with her husband in New Orleans, where she does most of her writing in a penthouse that affords a panoramic view of that intriguing, history-rich city.

Hazelhurst High School
Cordially Invites You To Attend
Your Ten Year Class Reunion,
Saturday, The Third of August
Eight O'Clock In The Evening
Hazelhurst Country Club
Hazelhurst, Ohio

Evening Attire   RSVP

Prologue

Ryder Hayes swung off his motorcycle and stared up at the old brick building. Ten years ago he'd said goodbye to this two-bit town. He had left as "that no-good boy from The Creek" and had promised himself he wouldn't come back.

But here he was, a success, in a position now to judge those who'd judged him, a position to shake up neat little worlds. Yet it seemed nothing had changed, that he hadn't changed.

Ryder slipped off his helmet and hung it on one of the bike's handlebars. He tunneled his fingers through his hair, damp from the heavy helmet. Squinting against the sun, he surveyed the campus he remembered so well.

Hazelhurst High. Ryder hooked his thumbs in the back pockets of his faded jeans. It was as ugly, as desolate a structure as it had been when he left. The brick looked aged and sad; the school board still hadn't seen fit to shell out a few bucks for some trees or bushes. He lifted his lips in cynical amusement. But when had the school board ever been interested in the students?

Ryder turned away from the building and started for the stadium. He reached it in two, maybe three minutes—there was nothing between it and the school but a small, paved parking lot—and climbed the ramp to the first level. No expense had been spared here. The rickety wooden bleachers had been exchanged for concrete ones even before his time at Hazelhurst High, and sometime since, the old scoreboard had been replaced by a new, computerized one.

He stared down at the empty stadium. As he did, he pictured it full, the crowd cheering wildly as Sonny Keighton, Hazelhurst's golden boy and Ryder's best friend, raced down the field for yet another touchdown.

Best friends, Ryder thought, his lips twisting again. At eighteen those two words meant everything; at nearly thirty he knew they meant nothing.

He turned his attention to another place on the field, a place where three girls wearing royal-blue-and-white uniforms had cheered their hearts out. A blonde, a brunette and a redhead, the three most popular girls at Hazelhurst High. But only one had mattered to him.

Jennifer.

With his mind's eye he could see her laughing as she urged the crowd on, see her smile and wave when she caught sight of him. And he could hear her slightly husky voice, the easiness of her laugh. But most of all, he could feel her against him, passionate and pliant and out of control.

Ryder swore and swung away from the field. Even after all this time thinking of her was like a blow to his gut. She'd given him the benefit of the doubt when no one else would give him the time of day, and she'd broken his heart.

He'd never been able to forget her.

He swore again and started down the ramp. Why had he come back? He could have refused the assignment. He'd proved himself valuable enough to Lansing International that turning down the job at the Hazelhurst plant wouldn't have weakened his position in the corporation.

He stepped from the shade of the ramp into the harshness of the noonday sun. Who was he kidding? He knew exactly why he'd come back—to see her, Jennifer.

To see her and drum her out of his head.

Ryder swung onto the big black bike and kicked back the center stand. Earlier he'd thought that nothing in Hazelhurst had changed. He'd been wrong. Something here would have surely changed—Jennifer Joyce would little resemble the girl who played havoc with his memory. That girl had never really existed; she'd been nothing more than an adolescent's dream of the perfect girl and of fitting in.

Ryder pulled his helmet on, opened the throttle and turned the key. The bike's engine roared to life. He was beyond silly adolescent dreams. He knew who—

and what—he was. By the time he finished his assignment and left Hazelhurst, the past would be nothing more than a bad memory.

And Jennifer Joyce would be firmly affixed there.

Chapter One

It couldn't be him.

Jennifer Joyce stood in the doorway to her father's office, staring at the man behind the desk, not believing her eyes. It couldn't be Ryder...it couldn't be, but it was.

Heart thundering in her chest, she moved her gaze slowly over him. Ryder had come back. He didn't have to look up from the papers he studied for her to know. Everything about the man called to her memory of the boy—the way he held himself, relaxed and controlled at the same time, the way his dark brown hair fell across his high forehead, the cocky tilt of his head.

But there were things that were different, she acknowledged, placing her hand on the doorjamb for support. His hairline had receded just a little, creating arches at his temple that mirrored the shape of his eyebrows, eyebrows that had already given his face a devilish look. She could see, even though he sat, that he'd filled out. His body, his face, looked strong, manly. Gone was any softness or curve of youth that had existed at eighteen, both having been replaced by angles and sinew in maturity.

The tie loosely knotted at the throat of his chambray shirt was new, too, and a surprise. Casual though it was, he'd once said he'd never become a "suit" like her father. His idea of dress wear had been an old denim jacket with an American flag appliquéd across the back.

Except for once. The thought jumped to her mind before she could stop it. She pushed it away and lowered her eyes to his hands. He wore a gold watch that looked expensive, too expensive for a boy from The Creek, especially one who had left town with nothing, not even his high school diploma.

A trembling sensation started in the pit of Jennifer's stomach and spread until her hands shook so badly it was all she could do to slip them into the pockets of her navy linen trousers. Age had done nothing but made him more appealing. The years had added strength and character to a face that had already been wickedly handsome.

She must have made some sound, or maybe Ryder had sensed her presence, because he looked up then without evidence of any of the surprise she'd felt. Their eyes met. His were as brilliant a blue as she remembered, his mouth as finely cut and full as before.

Her heart, which had been beating crazily, stopped altogether for a moment before starting again with a vengeance. The last time she'd seen him he had been a boy, pale and bruised and hurting. His face had been bandaged, his expression defiant. Now he was a man, vigorous and confident and totally in control. And now, his expression gave nothing away.

Seconds ticked past. Warmth eased up her spine. Jennifer told herself to say something, but her mouth refused to move. Her past was staring her in the face and all she could do was gape. Then he smiled. The curving of his lips was slow, cynical and unabashedly sexy, and her knees turned to pudding.

She silently swore. She remembered that smile and, just as vividly, that he'd always been able to melt her with it. Unfortunately, it seemed he hadn't forgotten that fact, either.

"Hello, J.J."

Jennifer stiffened as his voice rippled over her. "Don't call me that."

Ryder arched one sweeping dark eyebrow. "Why? Because that was Sonny's pet name for you?"

That he could mention Sonny that way, so coolly, so callously, infuriated her. Didn't he feel any guilt at all? She tossed her head back. "No. Because my name's Jennifer."

He pushed back from the desk and stood. She saw then that his tie shouldn't have fooled her—he was wearing jeans, formfitting and ancient from wear. "You didn't mind at eighteen."

"There were a lot of things I didn't mind at eighteen that I couldn't stomach now."

"Is that so?" Ryder looked her over leisurely, insolently, then returned his gaze to hers.

Heat stung her cheeks. Jennifer told herself it was anger's sting, not remembering's, not the past's. "Yes."

Ryder came around the desk, and she fought the urge to back up. He stopped only inches from her. With all the odors of the factory, her father's pipe and the deodorizer hung above the door, she could still smell him. He smelled of leather and soap...and something she recognized as Ryder but couldn't identify. Whatever it was, it plucked at her memory and left her weak-kneed and breathless.

"You've changed your hair," he said softly, reaching out and touching just the tips of her chin-length pageboy. "It's shorter, parted on the side instead of the middle." He rubbed the ends between his fingers. "I like it."

Jennifer tipped her head so the strands slipped from his fingers. "A lot changes in ten years."

The sound he made was soft but edged with something hard. "Yeah, and a lot can change in a minute...or stay the same forever." He tucked his hands into the pockets of his faded jeans. "How about you, Jen? Have you changed more than your hair and clothes? Or are you the same bubbly little joiner you were in high school?"

"Let's just say I'm older, wiser and not nearly so gullible. Can you say the same?"

Ryder laughed in a way that was masculine and anything but amused. "It doesn't take twice for me to learn a lesson, and I was wise long before we ever met. You tend to get that way when your daddy uses your face for a punching bag."

Jennifer's heart constricted. Murmured words, soft and comforting, flew to her tongue. She swallowed them. Ten years ago she'd stopped feeling sympathy—or anything else—for Ryder Hayes. "It seems there are advantages to every situation. It took me a lot longer."

"So, you have changed." Ryder narrowed his eyes, the expression in them cool and more than a little dangerous. "When did it happen, Jen? The first time you didn't get something you wanted?"

She met his steely look with one of her own. "The night of the senior prom."

"The night you wanted to make love."

She sucked in a sharp breath. "I didn't."

"You did. It almost happened." Ryder lowered his eyes to her mouth, his voice to a caress. "Don't you remember, I stopped us. If not for that, we—"

"Your memory's faulty. I never *wanted* to make love with you." Jennifer swung away from him, guilt and shame gnawing at her.

Ryder caught her arms and turned her back around, being neither rough nor careful with her. "There are a lot of things about me that can be faulted, Jen." He slid his hand down her arm until he caught hers. He laced their fingers. "But not my memory. Not when it comes to remembering you . . . remembering us."

Jennifer stared at their joined hands, her heart thundering in her chest. She wanted to shout that there'd never been any "us." But she couldn't lie because they both knew the truth. Although it had always been Sonny back then, there had been something between them; Jennifer and Ryder, and it was be-

tween them still. Chemistry. Electricity. Whatever she
wanted to call it, even now it danced along her nerve
endings and crackled in the air between them.

Jennifer shook off his hand. She wasn't a girl anymore, and she wouldn't be controlled by something as
shoal as chemistry. "What are you doing in my father's office?"

"I'm surprised he didn't call you with the news."
Ryder's smile was small and satisfied. "For the time
being he's sharing an office with Billy Hayes's boy.
Local hero and local loser. Ironic, isn't it?"

"Sharing his office?" Jennifer repeated, looking
around the familiar room. There was nothing different about it, nothing that would suggest change. Except for Ryder's presence. "When did this happen?"

"Today." Ryder leaned against the edge of the desk,
relaxed, confident. He cocked an eyebrow. "Corporate headquarters sent me. A surprise package of
sorts."

Jennifer's mouth went dry, her palms damp. "What
are you saying, that you work for Lansing International?"

"That's exactly what I'm saying." Ryder picked up
a pencil. He tapped it against his thigh for a moment,
then stopped and looked at her. "I'm a controller for
Lansing. I've been sent to determine the profitability
of the Hazelhurst plant."

"A controller?"

Ryder smiled. "Some, your father included, will call
me a corporate ax man. I suspect I'm not going to be
much more popular with the good folks of Hazelhurst this time around than I was last."

Ryder had returned to settle the score.

Jennifer's breath caught. She took a step back, panic threading through her. What better way than to wreak revenge on the man who had been his father's boss? And how better could he hurt Hazelhurst than by destroying its largest job supplier?

Her father. Jennifer glanced around the office once again. He'd been plant manager here for as long as she could remember; his job was who he was. What would he do if... She couldn't finish the thought and looked back at Ryder. "Why are you doing this?"

"I'm only doing my job, Jennifer. Nothing more."

She shook her head. "Do you expect me to believe that? After everything, do you expect me to believe you?"

His expression hardened. "I see some things about you haven't changed." He tossed the pencil down. "You don't have a choice. All you get is my word that I'll be fair."

"Where is he?" she asked quietly.

"Who?" Ryder lifted his brows, all innocence.

"You know who I—" She took a deep breath. "My father, where is he?"

Ryder shrugged. "Daddy didn't tell me where he was going."

And neither did she. Without another word, Jennifer turned and left the office.

She wouldn't cry, she told herself, hurrying down the hallway that led from Hazelhurst Tool and Die's executive offices to the main shop. She would talk to her father. Surely it wasn't as bad as Ryder had led her to believe.

As she neared the shop, the sounds of the machines grinding, cutting and punching steel became louder. With them came the acrid scent of metal and grease and sweat.

Jennifer wrinkled her nose and, without looking around, let herself out. She'd never liked the factory and had never felt comfortable here. And today she wanted to run to her car instead of walk.

She settled for hurrying, pulling first her keys, then her sunglasses from her purse as she did. She reached the car, opened the door and slipped inside. Only then did she glance back. There was something depressing about the place, something that lacked humanity. The building was heavy and gray despite the landscaping designed to brighten it. The people inside worked long hours without sunshine or, for the most part, the benefit of human companionship.

But her father loved it. She started the car and backed out of the parking space. Twenty years ago he'd come to Hazelhurst, saved this plant from closing and become an instant hero. He could do it again, despite Ryder Hayes.

With that reassuring thought, she went to find him.

Her parents' house and the plant were located on opposite sides of town, but even so it took her barely twenty minutes to get there. Jennifer pulled up in front of the two-story frame house and smiled. She didn't know why she'd worried—her father's car was parked in the driveway, he'd no doubt come home for a late lunch.

The lilacs were blooming, and as she stepped out of the car she drew in their delicate but unmistakable scent. Funny how, even though she'd moved out years ago, she still thought of this house, this east-side neighborhood, as her home.

She followed the brick walk up, then crossed the wide front porch to the door. "Mom, Dad, it's me, Jen." She swung open the door and stepped inside.

As it always had, the house smelled like her mother's baking. Today, Jennifer thought, sniffing, she would find fresh-baked bread on the counter.

Her mother came out of the kitchen. "Jennifer, honey, what are you doing here?"

"I came to see Dad," Jennifer said, tipping her head, looking at her mother with concern. Not one of her silvering hairs was out of place, her smile was as crisp as her white apron, but still she looked shaken. "He is here?"

The older woman wiped her hands on her apron. "Of course. I was making lunch... have you eaten?"

Jennifer followed her mother into the kitchen. "No, but I don't think I could eat a..." Her words trailed off when she saw her father. Sitting stiffly at the table, his face was set in grim lines, and his usually robust complexion looked mottled.

Jennifer shifted her gaze from him to her mother. Mary Joyce, the woman known throughout Hazelhurst for her calm, was fluttering nervously around the kitchen. The unease she'd felt at the plant stole over her once again. *What if this time her father couldn't fix it?*

Jennifer fought the emotion and the thought. She cleared her throat. "Dad, I stopped at... the plant—" She looked at her mother again, helplessly.

"I'd stopped to see if you wanted to join me for lunch."

He looked at her then, and Jennifer winced at the fury in his eyes. "You saw . . . him?"

"In your office, yes." Jennifer sank into the chair kitty-corner to his. "He said corporate sent him. That he's a—"

"Corporate ax man? Did he tell you that?"

"Yes," she said softly. "In a way he said exactly that. What's going on, Dad? Is it as bad as—"

"Jennifer," her mother interrupted, slathering mayonnaise on bread as if her life depended on it, "you need to eat. How about a ham sandwich? I baked that sourdough bread you like so much."

Food, the cure for all ills. Jennifer swallowed a sigh and shot her mother a smile. "Sure, Mom. That sounds good." She turned back to her father. "Did you call headquarters?"

"You bet I did. They confirmed sending Hayes, then told me to cooperate! You'd think after thirty-two years of service they'd give me a little more credit."

Jennifer laid a hand on his arm; it was rock hard under her fingers. She squeezed. "Lansing wants to close the plant?"

He stood and crossed to the window. "They're thinking about it. That's why they sent that boy."

"How in the world," her mother said, crossing to the table and placing a pitcher of iced tea and a bag of chips there, "did that boy end up in such a position of authority? I can't imagine."

Jennifer could. Ryder had had everything going against him, but he'd never been stupid or lazy. He'd done well in his classes even though she'd never seen him take home a book.

No, she wasn't at all surprised at Ryder's success, only at his need for revenge.

"I just don't understand it," her father continued. "Sure our figures haven't been great, but we're still making money. And that's saying a lot what with today's inflated cost of labor, aging equipment and with the economy being in the toilet for the past couple of years. We've already laid off ten percent of our people...it just doesn't seem..."

His voice trailed off and, fighting tears, Jennifer stared at his back. She hated to see him like this. He'd always been so strong, so vigorous and indestructible. He'd always been the one to soothe and protect. Even during the darkest days after Sonny's death, he'd helped her. Now, for the first time, she had the sense that he was as human as the rest of the world...and that he needed her.

And she had no idea what to say.

She cleared her throat. Even so, when she spoke her voice was huskier than usual. "Is there anything I can do?"

Henry Joyce turned then, sending her the broad, confident smile that had always made her feel warm and protected. "Don't worry about me, baby girl. I said it myself, our figures aren't that bad. Probably the worst that will happen is they'll implement a few irritating changes. We'll all complain, tighten our belts and everything will blow over."

''See there,'' her mother said, setting the plates on the table. ''Nothing to worry about. And that's enough shop talk, you two. Let's have a pleasant lunch together, shall we?'' She passed her husband the bag of corn chips, then turned to Jennifer. ''I saw the perfect dress for your class reunion in the window of Sinclaire's. It's in that raspberry color you wear so well. I thought about putting it on hold for you to...''

Jennifer closed her office door behind her and crossed to the desk. The rest of her visit with her parents had passed under the guise of normalcy. *Guise* was right. Her mother's voice had been overbright, her father's expression troubled. For herself, the last thing she'd wanted to think about, let alone discuss, was her ten-year high school reunion.

Jennifer sighed and sank into her chair. Until today, even though she'd headed up the planning committee, she'd been pretty successful at both.

Ryder was back.

Jennifer leaned her head against the chair's headrest and closed her eyes. She'd thought she would never see him again. The day of Sonny's funeral he'd checked out of East Side General Hospital and disappeared.

But not before she'd gone to see him. She pressed the heels of her hands against her temple, futilely wishing—for maybe the billionth time—that she hadn't. Or that she couldn't remember the last scene between them.

But their every word, his every expression was burned into her brain. It had been as unforgettable as it had been ugly. The image of Ryder's bruised face, set as if chiseled from rock, filled her head. He hadn't defended himself to her, hadn't denied even one of her accusations. And although his face had been stony, his eyes... his eyes had been hurt and somehow accusing.

Jennifer swore and jumped up. She crossed to her files, yanked open the top drawer and began flipping through the folders. He'd had no right to look at her like that. She hadn't done anything wrong. All she'd been was too trusting, too good a friend to him.

And not enough of one to Sonny.

Jennifer pulled three files out of the drawer and tossed them on top of the cabinet. She needed to get busy. The day had already slipped by and she'd accomplished almost nothing. Tomorrow would be hectic. She had several showings. The Petersons had finally decided to put their plum of a house on the market, and she'd promised to stop by. She had a lunch meeting at the chamber of commerce, and there were still a thousand details to be taken care of for the reunion.

The reunion. Ryder. Jennifer sighed and rested her forehead against the open drawer, the pretense of working suddenly seeming as silly as it was futile. She softly shut the drawer and turned back to her desk.

She couldn't outrun the past, not this time.

It was here.

Chapter Two

All those years ago...

Her prom dress had been chiffon, done in a shoulderless style that hugged her waist and hips and whispered when she moved. Its color had been peach, not any ordinary mixture of orange and white, but rather one of those peaches that was so delicate, so translucent it had seemed to glow.

In the last hours before the day of her prom arrived, Jennifer ran her finger along the butterfly-soft fabric. She'd never worn anything so feminine or fussy, and she'd only agreed to the dress because her mother had wanted so badly for her to have it. Jennifer dropped her hand. And ever since, she'd dreaded the moment she would have to put it on, because she would feel as if she were trying to be something—someone—she wasn't.

She turned away from the dress, her eyes going almost unwittingly to the poster mounted on the wall beside her bed. It was a blowup of a photograph of her and her two best friends, Cyndi Saint and Meredith Robbins, taken while cheering the final game of the football season.

They were—and had been almost all through high school—the most popular girls in their class. Cyndi was the prettiest one, the most poised; Meredith the smartest, class valedictorian and recipient of a full scholarship to Vassar; she, well, she was good old Jennifer, everybody's friend.

Jennifer caught her bottom lip between her teeth, still staring at the poster. But good old Jennifer didn't wear dresses that looked like peach frosting or get her hair done at a beauty parlor. And the girl dubbed "Everybody's Friend" wouldn't yearn in her heart of hearts for her best friend's steady.

Jennifer tore her gaze away from the image of her and her friends and flipped off the closet light. She tiptoed back to her bed and, shivering against the predawn air, pulled the covers up around her chin.

Tomorrow was going to be a big day. As head of the prom committee she would have to check every detail of the dance and after-party. She would be running from early morning until the moment she left for the prom. If she didn't rest she would be a wreck.

Sighing, Jennifer leaned her head against the pillows she had propped up behind her. She didn't know if it was excitement or nerves causing her sleeplessness, but whichever, it looked as if she would be sporting dark circles tomorrow night because tonight there was no way she was going to sleep.

That fact acknowledged, Jennifer reached for the bottle of nail lacquer she'd set on her night table after applying a first coat only minutes ago. She turned it over in her hands. The color was called Just Peachy, it and its corresponding lip gloss were the exact shade of her dress.

She frowned, staring at the bottle. Everything didn't feel "just peachy." In fact everything felt weird. Meredith and Cyndi had been acting strange: Meredith withdrawn, Cyndi jittery and on edge. Both had seemed to be avoiding her and, at the last minute, had even backed out on the preprom party they'd planned months ago.

Jennifer shook her head, uncertain if she did so in denial of their behavior or her own hurt. Nerves, she told herself. They were all facing the future, the unknown and goodbye. After the prom would be graduation, after graduation they would all go their separate ways.

They'd all been afflicted, even Sonny.

Sonny. The bittersweet ache Jennifer felt every time she thought of Sumner Franklin Keighton III, captain of the football team and everything else at Hazelhurst High, settled over her. Breathing past the lump in her throat, she rested her head against the pillows once more.

She remembered the exact moment she'd fallen in love with him. It had been the fall of her sophomore year and a glorious autumn day. He'd strutted onto the football field, the sun glinting off his golden hair, looking every inch like one of the Saxon warriors they were studying in history class.

Jennifer smiled to herself. Sonny had never done anything to change her original impression of him. He was strong and confident, the kind of leader you could look up to and depend on. In his junior year he took the Hazelhurst Blue Swarm from trailing the league to leading it. Then he did it again this year. A real hero.

Although all the girls at Hazelhurst High had, at one time or another, giggled about how gorgeous Sonny Keighton was, Jennifer had never revealed the extent of her feelings for him. It had felt too personal—as if exposing those feelings would have been to totally expose herself. Maybe she'd even feared everyone would laugh at the idea of tomboy Jennifer and Mr. Everything. So she'd kept it her secret.

She'd been thankful for that decision ever since, because the summer after their junior year Sonny and Cyndi had finally, after dating on and off for years, started going steady.

Jennifer shook her head, not wanting to think about Sonny but being unable to stop—just as she'd been unable to stop loving him even though he belonged to Cyndi.

She had tried. She'd hidden her feelings from him, from her friends and family, but hiding them hadn't made them go away, and one afternoon in October he'd shown up at her house ''just to talk.''

That conversation had led to many, and Jennifer had learned that she and Sonny had a lot in common. They were both active and liked participating in and viewing a variety of sports. They were both outgoing and friendly and preferred lots of people and action to quiet and cozy.

Jennifer plucked at her flowery coverlet—another of the feminine touches in her life that her mother had insisted upon. Sonny didn't try to make her into something she wasn't, nor did he ridicule her tomboyish ways. If anything, he seemed to appreciate them.

Jennifer glanced back at the poster, focusing on the image of Cyndi, acknowledging guilt. Even though, in all the months that had passed and all the time she and Sonny had spent together, nothing had happened between them, more and more she caught him looking at her in a way he should have reserved for Cyndi. And several times lately she'd sidestepped moves she knew would have ended in an embrace.

The guilt ate at her and Jennifer lowered her eyes to her hands. Sure, each time she'd dodged his advance, but a part of her—a big part—had regretted doing so. What kind of friend was she? And what kind of friend would experience a bloom of hope when, as he'd begun to do, Sonny expressed dissatisfaction with Cyndi?

"J.J.," he would say, using his pet name for her, "I just don't feel comfortable with Cyndi. I can't talk to her like I talk to you. We don't like to do the same things. I don't even know why we're together."

Sonny was going to break up with Cyndi. Jennifer pulled her knees to her chest and rested her forehead on them. She didn't know what to do or how she should feel—on the one hand she felt like a traitor, on the other she trembled with hope.

She sighed. Maybe it didn't even matter, because after tonight nothing would ever be the same again.

Tears sprang to her eyes, and Jennifer blinked against them. She was the strong one, the one people came to for advice, a shoulder, a laugh. Tears weren't for her. But here they were, and who could she turn to for a shoulder or a smile?

"Psst... Jen... Jennifer..."

At the sound of her own name, Jennifer lifted her head and looked around the dark room. Just as she thought she'd imagined it, gravel sprayed against her window.

Sonny, Jennifer thought, her heart rapping against her chest. She climbed out of bed and crept to the partially open window, being especially quiet as her parents' room was directly below hers and the old floorboards creaked. Gravel tapped against her window once more before she reached it.

There, she slid the window up a little farther and peered at the ground below. Just as she opened her mouth to call his name, a shadow separated itself from the huge old oak tree beside the house. Her first feeling was of disappointment; the boy standing below her window was dark instead of fair, her friend instead of her love. "Ryder," she whispered, "it's you."

"Were you expecting someone else?"

Her cheeks heated. From the tone of his voice she almost thought he knew who she'd wished he was. But of course, he couldn't know.

"Cat got your tongue, Jen?"

"Of course not." She shook her head. "I'm surprised, that's all. It *is* the middle of the night, Ryder."

"I need to talk to you."

"I don't think that's a good idea, my parents—"

"Don't sweat it." He shot her his cocky just-watch-me smile and jumped, catching the lowest branch of the tree and swinging himself up. Hardly rustling a leaf, he made his way from branch to branch until they faced each other.

For long moments she just stared at him, the pulse throbbing in her head until she was dizzy from it. He looked different tonight, serious, not at all like the wicked tease she'd seen that afternoon at school, the boy who had leaned against the side of the gymnasium, smoking cigarettes with his buddies and whistling at freshman girls as they passed.

"What's wrong?" she asked finally, breathlessly. "Is it your father? Has he..." Her words trailed off as his gaze lowered. Her nipples were hard and pressed boldly against her thin cotton gown. She crossed her arms over her chest even as a funny little tingle trailed up her spine.

"You're cold," he murmured, his voice thick. "Here, take my jacket."

Even as she protested, he shrugged out of the old denim jacket, the one her mother hated so much because it had an American flag appliquéd across the back. The sixties having happened or not, her mother still thought he should be arrested.

Jennifer slipped it on. It was warm from his body and smelled of tobacco and riding against the wind.

She suddenly felt feminine and ridiculously safe. "What did you want to tell me?"

"I'm going to pick you up tonight."

"But, Ryder, we'd decided I would—"

"It's not right for you to pick me up for the prom, Jen." His thick dark hair fell across his forehead, and he pushed impatiently at it. "I'm the guy, the guy pays and drives. That's the way it is."

"That's silly." She drew in a quick breath. "I don't care about—"

"I do." He touched the curve of her cheek just once, lightly, then dropped his hand. The spot seemed to burn from his touch, and Jennifer told herself the late hour was affecting her. "I want this night to be special for you."

She caught his hand, unreasonably alarmed. "You promised me you wouldn't ride your bike tonight, even to pick me up. You gave me your word, Ryder."

He looked down at their joined hands, then back at her. "Have I ever broken a promise to you?"

"No, but—"

"God, you're beautiful."

Jennifer's stomach flip-flopped even as she slipped her hand from his. She moved a fraction back from the window. "Ryder, we're friends."

He laughed tightly. "Don't worry, babe, I'm not trying to start anything." He trailed his gaze over her. "But you are beautiful, you know. And don't say it."

"What?"

"That Cyndi's the pretty one."

"She is."

"Yeah, with about as much life as a china doll. Drop that girl and she'd shatter into a billion pieces."

Guilt plucked at her. Angry at the feeling, she narrowed her eyes. "Don't say that. It's not nice."

"Nice?" Ryder mocked, raising his eyebrows. "Jen, boys like me don't say nice things."

Jennifer inched her chin up. "She's my friend."

"Is she?"

"I'm going in."

She drew back. He grabbed her hand and the leaves rustled. "Dammit, Jen. I'm sorry."

She glared at him a moment, then relaxed and smiled. She could never stay mad at Ryder, no matter how he infuriated her. "I know. But I've still got to go. My dad's a light sleeper."

"No kidding." Ryder lifted his lips in a cynical smile. "He's probably on his way out here right now with a chain saw and a rifle. I can see the headlines tomorrow—Local Hero Rids Hazelhurst of Riffraff. Mayor Awards Key To City."

Upset, Jennifer pulled her hand from his. "I hate it when you talk like that. It's not true, you're not like your dad."

His cynical smile faded, softened. Seconds ticked past. He stared at her intently, almost as if he were memorizing everything about her. A funny, trembling sensation settled in the pit of her stomach, and Jennifer folded her arms tighter around herself.

"Ryder?" She cleared her throat. "You sure you're okay? Nothing's...wrong?"

"No, not now." His voice was so husky it seemed more a rasp than a whisper. He leaned over and brushed his mouth against hers. His lips were warm, his chin scratchy. The blood rushed to her head until she thought she might faint.

He trailed a finger across her bottom lip. "Good night, Jen. Don't forget, I'll pick you up."

"I won't," she whispered even though he'd already started down the oak. He descended the tree as quietly as he'd ascended it. When his feet hit the ground he looked back up at her and smiled. Back was the bad boy of earlier that day, the irreverent, cocky kid who spent more time in the principal's office than in class. Her heart did a funny little dance.

"Thirteen hours, babe. And you're going to look like a princess. No doubt about it."

He turned and disappeared into the night. It wasn't until then that Jennifer realized she was still wearing his jacket.

Chapter Three

Jennifer wasn't quite sure how she got home. She'd slammed out of her office, not even taking the time to say good-night to her partner, Susan Jennings. In much the same way, she slammed out of her car now, racing for the front door of the east-side cottage she had bought then renovated almost on her own. Inside, she took the stairs two at a time and ran down the hall to the guest bedroom.

Panting, she stopped in front of the closet. Don't do this, she told herself. Don't look back.

She yanked open the closet door, anyway, then rifled through the garments to find one at the very back, one she hadn't looked at, hadn't touched, in many years.

As her fingers closed over the ancient denim, they started to tremble. Jennifer swore, sucked in a sharp breath and pulled the jacket from its hiding place.

She held the beat-up jacket in her hands. How many times during that summer after Sonny's death had she almost taken her mother's sewing shears to this? She'd wanted to burn it, she'd pummeled it with her fists, she'd stomped on it... and once, on a hot day late in August, she had curled up with it on the bed and sobbed—because Sonny was dead, because Meredith and Cyndi had deserted her and Ryder had betrayed her. She'd sobbed because there was nothing of her childhood left. Guilt and despair and anger had snatched the last of it away from her.

Now Jennifer brought it to her face. It still smelled like him. Ten years had passed, and pressing her face to this piece of clothing made her feel all the aches of eighteen again—especially the one only Ryder had been able to make her feel.

Jennifer squeezed her eyes shut against the pain, against the memories. Neither would leave her. Finally, tiredly, she let herself be dragged back.

The night of the prom, she'd turned this way and that in her bedroom mirror, admiring her reflection. Ryder had been right—she looked like a princess.

The dress fit her petite frame perfectly. Her shoulder-length auburn hair had been professionally done just an hour ago at both her mother's beauty parlor and pleading. Still parted in the middle, the front had been pulled back and pinned up, the ends were a riot of big, soft curls. At her throat, hung on a fine gold chain, was a crucifix made out of opals; at her ears, matching opal studs. Both had been early graduation presents.

What would Sonny think of the way she looked?

Jennifer colored at her own thought and stroked the filmy fabric. It didn't matter. He was Cyndi's date, Cyndi's boyfriend, not hers. She and Ryder would have a wonderful time together. It would be a night none of them would forget.

"You look beautiful."

Jennifer turned toward her mother. She stood in the doorway, wiping her hands on her apron and smiling. With her mother had come the smell of the fresh-baked brownies she'd made for the after-prom party.

"Are you sure?" Jennifer glanced critically back in the mirror. "This dress is so—"

"Flattering," her mother finished for her, crossing the room. She adjusted the dress's bodice, hiking it up a little. "Your father won't believe his eyes. You look so grown-up."

Jennifer smiled and turned back to her reflection. "I do, don't I?" She laughed then, whirling around. "I've been so busy I haven't had time to actually think about tonight. Now I can't wait!"

Her mother interrupted her laughter. "Jennifer, I need to talk to you. It's important."

Jennifer stopped, her smile fading. Her mother had retreated to the corner of the bed and was toying with the ruffled edge of her apron. Her mother always fidgeted and fluttered when she was nervous or upset. "What's up, Mom?"

Mrs. Joyce paused, then drew what sounded to Jennifer like a careful breath. "Your father and I just want to warn you to be careful tonight. You know we trust you and your judgment, but we're concerned—''

"You don't trust Ryder," Jennifer interrupted, heat staining her cheeks. "Because of his father and because he's from The Creek."

"That's not true, honey. Your father and I have never judged one person by another's sins."

"No? Then what's this all about?"

Her mother's still-unlined cheeks reddened. "Be honest, Jennifer Marie, that boy has a reputation for trouble all his own. We're your parents, we have a right to be concerned."

Jennifer thought of the comment Ryder had made early that morning and fought back a wave of anger. "Don't be. I'll be perfectly safe."

The older woman began pleating and repleating the stiff white cotton, her eyes never leaving her daughter's. "It's rumored that his father raises his hand to both his wife and children. I wouldn't say anything about this now but... that type of behavior runs in families."

Anger left Jennifer speechless—but for only a moment. She faced her mother. "I can't believe you said that! Ryder's not that way, Mom. He's not!"

"I'm sorry, honey. Of course he's not." She stood and crossed to her daughter, fussing with the curls that spilled over her shoulders. "But take some money just in case. And if you need anything, we'll be home all night."

"For Pete's sake, Mom, I'm driving."

Mrs. Joyce frowned and fooled with the dress's bodice again. "I know. I wish Cyndi and Sonny had wanted to double, or Meredith and that nice boy she's going with."

"Well, they didn't. They wanted their privacy."

"Are you sure it was...they...who wanted privacy?"

Jennifer bit back a smart answer and swung away from her mother. She crossed to the closet and grabbed the box that contained her new shoes, dyed the same Just Peachy shade as the rest of her outfit. She gritted her teeth as she yanked on one, then the other. She would bet neither Cyndi or Meredith was getting the third degree right now. Of course, both of them had respectable dates.

"You haven't answered my question, Jennifer."

Jennifer stood back up, looking her mother in the eyes, so angry her hands shook. "As far as I'm concerned, Mom, you didn't ask one."

"This is your big night, and I don't want to fight. But consider this from our point of view—you're a cheerleader, one of the most popular girls at school. You could have your pick of boys. Yet, you go everywhere with your 'friend' Ryder. Honey, we just don't understand."

And they never would. Jennifer tilted her chin up. "Ryder and I are just friends. Okay? You don't have a thing to worry about."

Her mother smiled a little and touched her daughter's cheek. "Okay, sweetie." Turning, she started for the door. "Better hurry, he'll be here any moment."

Jennifer watched her mother go, tears welling in her eyes. She hated disappointing her parents, but how could she explain that she didn't have her pick of the boys? That the only one she wanted was taken?

Blinking furiously against the tears, she stared sightlessly into the mirror. And what could she tell her mother or father about Ryder and why she consented—enjoyed—being paired with him?

Color crept up her face. She certainly couldn't tell them that he made her feel alive and free and somehow grown-up, or that he seemed wiser, more mature than the other boys at school. They'd never let her out of the house again. And if she told them he made her feel things she knew she shouldn't, things she'd given into on a few occasions, they would send her to Siberia.

Jennifer pressed her cool hands to her hot cheeks, confused and embarrassed by her own thoughts. What was it about Ryder? They were only friends. She loved Sonny. Why did he make her feel...so aware and aching, so out of control?

Meredith had once said that Ryder was one of those boys you look at and know he's just plain bad, that he'll bring you nothing but heartache and trouble, but you can't help but worry over your hair and makeup anyway—because you know it's wrong, because of the danger.

Meredith was so smart, Jennifer thought, maybe that *was* it. Maybe Ryder fascinated her because he was different, a little dangerous, a mystery. She wouldn't be the only one, she'd heard both Mary Lynn

Peterson and Lanie Meyers had succumbed to him—and had their hearts broken.

Jennifer tipped her chin up. She didn't have to worry about that. She may be fascinated, but the only one who could break her heart was Sonny.

From downstairs she heard several things simultaneously: the sound of the doorbell, the agitated barking of their scruffy cocker spaniel and the excited chatter of her equally scruffy younger brother.

Ryder was here.

A strange trembling started in the pit of her stomach, and her palms began to sweat. Jennifer crossed to the window and peeked out. The only vehicle in the driveway was her parents' new Buick. Ryder's big black motorcycle was nowhere in sight. He'd kept his promise.

After taking one last glance in the mirror, she started for the door and the biggest evening of her life.

The trip down the hall to the head of the stairs took only seconds. There, she stopped, heart thundering in her chest. Ryder stood at the bottom with her parents, a florist's box in his hand. She trailed her gaze over him. He looked...magnificent.

Jennifer lifted a hand to her chest, to her runaway heart, and sucked in a steadying breath. She hadn't expected him to wear a tuxedo. Not Ryder. Not the rebel who broke dress codes just on principle. She'd expected him, maybe, in a tux jacket with a T-shirt and jeans underneath. Maybe worse. They'd never discussed it.

But here he was, outfitted in an elegant black tuxedo with all the trimmings.

Jennifer started down the stairs, one hand on the banister, the other holding up the skirt's sea of fabric. He looked up then and her heart, which had been beating out of control, stopped altogether.

His blue gaze was as intense, as penetrating, as always, but tonight there was something in it that made her feel like the most beautiful girl in the world.

He held out his hand; she took it. His fingers were warm, almost hot, to her own cool ones. He smiled at her, a small curving of his lips that spoke of camaraderie and of secrets.

"For you," Ryder murmured, handing her the florist's box.

She opened it. Nestled inside was a traditional pin-on corsage—the single flower an exquisite white orchid. Jennifer lifted her gaze from the flower to his eyes, her throat closing over the words she knew she should say. The exotic choice both stunned and touched her. It made her feel, somehow, as if she were wearing the right dress after all.

The moment was broken as her mother stepped in and, after much experimentation, insisted on pinning the corsage to her evening bag. The whole while her mother fussed over the flower, her father clicked photographs and her brother made disgusting little-boy sounds while he ran in circles around them.

By the time they left the house, Ryder's expression was tight, and Jennifer wondered if she had only imagined those moments of electricity between them.

As they stepped out of view of her parents, Ryder held out his hand. "Keys."

Jennifer handed them over without comment. He helped her into the car, then went around to the driver's side. After he'd backed out of the driveway and started up the street, she turned to him. "Sorry about my parents and all the pictures. They're kind of embarrassing sometimes."

He didn't take his eyes from the road. "It's cool, Jen. No big deal."

She noticed then the muscle that jumped in his jaw. Her stomach sank. Had her father said something to him? She could just imagine him down there putting the fear of God into Ryder. She cleared her throat. "How'd you get here?"

"Hitched."

She widened her eyes. "Wearing a tux?"

"Yeah." His lips tilted. "A lady with a station wagon full of groceries picked me up right away. Told me all about her senior prom."

"She sounds nice." Jennifer folded and refolded a bit of chiffon. "What did your parents think about all this?" As soon as the question passed her lips, she wished she could take it back. But she couldn't, and she saw Ryder flex his fingers on the steering wheel.

"There might have been a glimmer of something in my mother's eyes, but she's so tired I don't think she feels much of anything anymore. But my old man—" Ryder took a corner too fast "—it made his day."

Jennifer swallowed past the lump in her throat. "You didn't have to...do all this, Ryder. It wasn't necessary."

He angled her a glance. In that moment she thought she saw something soft, even wishful, in his expression. Then it was gone. "Yeah, it was. It's your prom, it's a big deal." He laughed. "Maybe someday you'll pick up some kid wearing a tux and tell him all about tonight."

Jennifer frowned. "It's your prom too, Ryder."

He met her eyes, all traces of amusement—cynical or otherwise—gone. "No, Jen. It's not."

In a funny way she'd understood exactly what he meant.

If only she hadn't. Jennifer looked down at the denim jacket clutched in her hands. If only she hadn't felt his isolation so keenly. Hating him now would be so much easier.

She sighed and sank to the bed, bringing the fabric to her face once again. That night, its events, had haunted her for ten years. How, she wondered as she had countless times since, had it affected Cyndi and Meredith?

Lying back against the mattress, Jennifer stared at the ceiling and let her mind once more go careening back ten years.

The entire prom committee had eaten at the country club where the dance was being held. Ryder had had nothing in common with any of them and had grown quieter as the meal progressed. And the quieter he'd grown, the more effervescent she had become.

Still, she had thought everything was going to be okay until one of the kids had made a crack about Ryder's father. The night had disintegrated from that point on.

Jennifer drew her eyebrows together. She remembered that the kid had been wearing a baby-blue tux, although she couldn't recall his name.

"Hey, Ryder," he'd called, "is your old man going to be at the after-party? Maybe he'll spike the punch for us."

There had been a moment of absolute quiet as everyone turned to Ryder. He pushed slowly away from the table, pinning the other boy with his narrowed eyes. Jennifer's stomach crashed to her toes—Ryder had been rumored to fight over less.

Several seconds of pregnant silence passed, then just as the boy started to squirm, Ryder smiled. "Count on it, man. He wouldn't miss it for the world."

Everyone laughed and went on as if nothing had happened. Ryder too seemed unaffected, every inch the cool, impenetrable dude he was reputed to be. Jennifer knew better—she felt his fury and his alienation as keenly as if it were her own.

She released a shaky breath and laid a hand on his arm, hoping to comfort him. He stepped away from her touch. "I'm going for a smoke," he muttered, and without looking at her, turned and walked away.

Jennifer watched him go, tears stinging the back of her eyes. Why did people have to be so cruel, so thoughtless? She almost wished, even though she knew it wouldn't have solved anything, that Ryder had pounded the insensitive little nerd silly.

She blinked against the tears. If only they could go back to the moment she'd walked down the stairs at her house and taken his hand. The evening had seemed so bright then, so full of promise.

Maybe they could. She would talk to him; she'd always been able to coax Ryder out of himself. Jennifer started to follow him, then stopped as another member of the prom committee called to her from the opposite doorway.

"Jen, better come quick, one of the banners fell and now the drummer refuses to play underneath it! He keeps muttering 'death trap, death trap.' I think he's on something!"

Jennifer took one last look in the direction Ryder had gone, sighed and turned toward her classmate. She would handle this crisis, then find Ryder. Everything would be fine.

That crisis led to another and another. By the time she set out to find Ryder, the band was already taking its first break.

Jennifer slipped through the still-thin crowd, greeting classmates in passing, stopping only when she absolutely couldn't get around it—which was more often than she liked. Everyone wanted to talk, to congratulate her on the decorations, comment on her dress. It was impossible for the girl voted Everybody's Friend to slip unnoticed through the crowd.

Jennifer broke away from several well-wishers, frowning as she scanned the room for Ryder. It would be easier to find him if she wasn't shorter than the majority of the people in the room or if the crystal chandeliers hadn't been dimmed to create an atmosphere conducive to romance. Likewise, the tables surrounding the dance floor were each adorned with miniature hurricane lamps nestled in pink and white carnations. Lots of mood, little light.

She glanced up at the stage as a couple of the band members began to strum their instruments, warming back up after the break. Above the stage was the re-hung and only slightly worse-for-wear banner announcing One Moment in Time, the prom's theme. To the side of the stage were tiers of ferns and potted pink and white azaleas.

Jennifer placed her hands on her hips in frustration. Could Ryder have left? She'd been busy for more than an hour, but surely he wouldn't have left her dateless and stranded. What would she do if—

Then she saw him. He was leaning against the stage, conversing with one of the band members. It looked to Jennifer as if they were more than passing acquaintances. Breathing a sigh of relief, she hurried toward him.

"Finally!" She smiled brilliantly at the musician before turning to Ryder. "I was looking all over for you."

"Really?" Ryder faced her, his expression furious.

Jennifer took a step back, surprised. The emotion that burned in his eyes was the result of more than a comment made by a geeky classmate. Was he angry at her for leaving him alone so long? That didn't sound like Ryder either, but what else could it be?

"I managed to save us one of the best tables." She touched his arm, pointing toward a small grouping of tables to the right of the stage.

"Fine. I'll be there in a minute."

Heat flooded her cheeks at both his curtness and the way he turned his back to her to resume his conversation with the musician. She touched his arm again.

"Cyndi and Sonny are already here. They're waiting for us."

"The king," he said slowly, swiveling to meet her gaze, "and queen . . . can wait."

Jennifer stepped back as if he'd slapped her and, without speaking, whirled around and started for the table. He caught her before she'd gone a dozen steps. His grip on her elbow was just shy of painful, and she stopped and glared at him. "I won't be treated that way, Ryder."

"You want respect? That's a two-way street, babe."

She tilted her chin up. "What's that supposed to mean?"

"You're *my* date," he said, his voice low and deceptively soft. "We may be 'only friends,' but tonight you're my date."

She jerked her arm from his grasp. "Then act like it."

"Don't push me, Jen." He leaned toward her until she felt his breath stir against her face. "We both know what will happen if you do."

She colored and took a step back. "What's gotten into you? I had responsibilities tonight beyond being your date. You knew about them."

"Yeah, but I didn't know—"

"Hey, you two," Sonny interrupted, coming up between them, his well-modulated voice as smooth as silk, "Cyndi and I are getting bored over here."

Ryder turned toward him, eyes narrowed. "Jen and I aren't the entertainment. That's what the band's for, Sonny. Go ask *your girl* to dance."

"Ryder!" Jennifer laid a hand on his arm and was shocked to discover his muscles were tensed, as if readied for a fight. She looked from one boy to the other. Where Ryder was dark and mysterious looking, Sonny was fair haired, the quintessential all-American boy. They looked, literally, like night and day.

These two—the golden boy and bad boy of Hazelhurst High—were best friends and had been for years. No one, including she, was sure why. But tonight something had changed. Animosity emanated from them as they faced each other, as did challenge.

And whatever they were battling for or against, at this point Sonny was winning. Jennifer could see it in his confident, slightly amused expression, and the opposite in Ryder's defiant and furious one.

"I don't know what's gotten into you two," Jennifer said crisply, "but tonight's our big night and I intend to have fun! Now, come on." Smiling, she slipped an arm through one of each boy's and steered them to the table.

When they reached it, Jennifer's spirits sank a smidgen. She had a bigger job than just cheering up the two guys. Cyndi, breathtaking in a deep rose gown, seemed tense and as breakable as the china doll Ryder had called her the night before. She smiled and greeted them all as they sat, but Jennifer noticed the smile didn't reach her eyes.

Moments passed, nobody spoke. Jennifer drew her eyebrows together, looking from one person to the next. Cyndi, obviously anxious, seemed to almost cling to Sonny; Sonny totally ignored her, seeming more interested in tapping his fingers in time to the music and looking around the ballroom. And all Ryder seemed able to do was glower at Sonny. She might as well have been invisible.

Nerves, Jennifer reassured herself, refusing to acknowledge the feeling that her world was falling apart. Everyone was on edge because high school was ending and the future was beginning. It was up to her to get things going.

"Doesn't Cyndi look gorgeous, Ryder? I wish I could wear that color, it's wonderful!" Jennifer turned to her friend. "And Cyndi, doesn't Ryder look great? Can you believe the tux? I almost died when I saw him!" Not even waiting for response, she plowed on. "Everyone seems to be enjoying the band, and I can't tell you how many people stopped me to comment on the ballroom."

Jennifer ignored her companions' deadpan expressions. "I wonder where Meredith and Craig are? Cyndi, do you know what time they were planning to get here?"

Cyndi shook her head, looking like the simple movement took extreme effort. "I haven't talked to her."

"I know they were having dinner in Crystal Lake—" Jennifer saw Sonny lift his head at that "—I told her we'd save a table and to look for us but..." Her words trailed off. Carrying on a conversation by herself was as uncomfortable as the silence. At least with silence, she didn't appear a bubbly little idiot.

"Ryder—" Jennifer jumped up and held out her hand "—let's dance." He hesitated until Sonny started to push away from the table as if he were about to claim her, then stood and took her hand.

They swung onto the dance floor to the sound of Dan Fogelberg's hit, "Longer." Jennifer moved into his arms, the top of her head barely reaching his chin. They'd danced like this a hundred times before, and she knew exactly what to expect. Unlike Sonny, who was an expert, there was nothing fancy about the way Ryder danced, he just pulled her close and moved to the music.

But there was a sureness about the way Ryder led— about the way he did everything—and she always felt relaxed and feminine in his arms. Even tonight when they were both on edge, she felt safe, secure.

Jennifer drew in his familiar scent and thought of the denim jacket tucked safely in the back of her closet so her mother wouldn't see it. She would have to give it back tomorrow.

She slipped her hands up to his shoulders, frowning as she discovered his muscles were rock hard under her fingers. "I'm sorry Curt made that comment about your dad. He can be a real jerk sometimes."

"Don't worry about it. I'm not."

"Then what's wrong?" she asked softly, tipping her head back to meet his eyes. "What's going on between you and Sonny?"

Ryder paused, searching her face with his penetrating blue gaze. "What's going on," he returned just as softly, "between Sonny and...Cyndi?"

Jennifer's heart stopped. He'd drawn the question out in a way that suggested he hadn't worded it quite as he'd wanted. "I don't know what you mean."

"Don't you?"

"No."

"I thought you and Cyndi were best friends."

"Why are you picking a fight with me?"

"See, you are observant."

She pulled out of his arms. "I'm sorry Curt said that about your father and I'm sorry I had to take care of prom details and that you're sorry you're here." Her voice cracked a little on the last. "But that's it, Ryder, I'm not apologizing for anything else tonight."

Ryder drew her back against his chest, closer than right for "friends." He rested his head on the top of hers, and she heard him draw in a deep breath. "Jen, if I asked you to leave now, with me, what would you say?"

"Oh, Ryder..." She squeezed her eyes shut, fighting the irrational urge to say yes. "Please, don't ask. I can't just le—"

"That's what I thought." He rubbed his chin against her hair then released her. "The music's stopped."

It had and they made their way back to the table, disappointment curling through her. Disappointment not with Ryder or his question, but with herself. She had the feeling she'd let him down and that, somehow, she would regret not giving in to her instinct to let him lead her away from here.

It was too late to change her mind, however. They'd reached the table, and Cyndi was looking at her in a way that made Jennifer want to hug her and tell her everything would be all right. She bit back a sigh and slipped into the chair Ryder held out for her.

No sooner had they taken their seats than Sonny smiled thinly at Ryder. "Enjoy your dance, buddy?"

"What's it to you?"

Sonny shook his head, his golden hair feathering across his forehead. "You've got an attitude problem tonight, man. It was a simple question." Sonny shifted his eyes to Jennifer. She thought she saw something in them she never had before. Then it was gone. "Who'd have thought Ryder Hayes would end up with one of the belles of the ball? Unbelievable isn't it?"

Ryder met his gaze evenly, unsmilingly, and Jennifer's blood went cold. "Couldn't have done it without you. Right, Sonny-boy?"

"That's what I like about you, man, credit where credit is due." Sonny leaned back in his chair as if he owned the world. "But I've got to tell you, you've about reached your limit."

"Is that so?" Ryder's voice was low and edged with something raw.

Jennifer shifted her gaze from one person to the next, her heart pounding. Cyndi looked as if she might be physically ill; the guys looked as if nothing would satisfy them but coming to blows.

Then she spotted Meredith and Craig, weaving through the crowd, heading in the opposite direction. Thank God for Craig's awful white tux, if not for it she might have missed them!

She jumped up. "Look, there they are!" After frantically waving for a moment, Jennifer acknowledged that there was no way the couple was going to see her. "I'll go get them," she said, then started across the room, moving faster than was wise in her high heels.

She had to practically lasso them to get them to the table and, even after all that, their addition didn't help much. Meredith, looking elegantly beautiful in her blue taffeta gown and softly curling hair, seemed as on edge as the rest of them. Jennifer tried to draw her out, but tonight her usually reserved friend was downright somber. At least Craig was talkative. He laughed and chatted with her about the band and what to expect at the party later, but after only a few minutes he asked Meredith to dance and they exited the table.

Hours slipped by in kaleidoscope fashion and finally, when she couldn't take any more of the guys' cutting remarks, Cyndi's nervous laughter or her own overbright chattering, she stood and motioned toward the opposite end of the ballroom, to a glass wall that faced the swimming pool and garden beyond. "I need some air. Join me, Ryder?"

Moments later they stepped through the glass doors and onto the deck that overlooked the pool. By unspoken but mutual consent, she and Ryder circled the pool and headed for the maze of paths that wound through the lush garden. The cloudy night offered little moonlight, and it would have been difficult to find their way had it not been for the illumination of the small lanterns placed every few feet along the pathway.

Jennifer heard the hiss of flame touching tobacco, the pull of Ryder's indrawn breath, then caught the slightly acrid scent of the smoke. Still they didn't speak, but kept walking until they'd reached the very center of the garden.

There, Jennifer stopped and turned toward him. "Why are you antagonizing Sonny?"

Ryder's laugh sounded anything but amused. He flicked his cigarette into the damp bushes. "Typical."

"And what's that supposed to mean?" She placed her fists on her hips and tipped up her chin.

For long seconds, Ryder stared at her, a muscle working in his jaw. Finally, softly, he said, "Sonny can't do anything wrong, can he? He's perfect in every way... the perfect son, athlete, boyfriend. An angel sent to bless all the good people of Hazelhurst."

"This isn't about Sonny."

"No?" He laughed again. "Isn't it all about Sonny? Everything we do and are... even us being here together is about him. Think of it, Jen, our world revolves around one eighteen-year-old boy. Blows you away, doesn't it?"

"I can't talk to you when you're like this. I'm going in."

He caught her arm as she turned to go. His gaze was hard with purpose. "What's sad is that you really *don't* know what I'm talking about."

"And I don't care, Ryder." She shook her head, several of her curls tumbling free with the movement. "Whatever your problem is—"

"Not my problem, babe. Yours and your friends'. The three of you buzz around Sonny like bees looking for nectar. You call yourselves friends—best friends—but the only thing you have in common is competition and keeping secrets, one secret in particular."

Jennifer tugged against his grasp, her cheeks on fire. "That's not true! We are friends!"

"You're three silly, little girls fluttering around one spoiled adolescent boy. I've watched you all for more than a year now, it's as amusing as it is ridiculous."

"Why are you saying this?" she cried, tugging against his hold on her arm. "Why are you trying to hurt me?"

"I'm not trying to hurt you...." He made a sound of exasperation, of frustration. "Jen, open up your eyes. Do you think Mr. Hazelhurst High doesn't know what's going on, that he doesn't egg you on. He plays the three of you off each other like—"

"Let me go, Ryder!" Something in his words nagged at her; she fought against it and him. "Let me go or I'll scream, I swear I will."

"Why are you getting so upset, Jen? Is it because you know I'm right? Is it because—"

"Stop it!" When Jennifer drew back to slap him, he caught her hand and hauled her against his chest. He held her there for a moment, his breath as ragged as hers, his heart as out of control.

"Is Sonny what you want, Jennifer?" he asked finally, his voice soft and thick. "Does he make you ache like I do? Can he make you lose control until all you can do is feel and all you want is to make love?" Ryder slipped his hands down her back until he cupped her. "Haven't you ever asked yourself why it's like this between us?"

"Don't do this, Ryder." She pushed against his chest, panic warring with arousal. "Let me go."

"Why?" He trailed his lips lightly across her temple. "You know I won't hurt you. What are you afraid of?"

"I'm...not," she whispered brokenly, already lost.

"You are," he murmured, pressing his lips to her throat, to the pulse she knew beat wildly there. "You're afraid of the way I make you feel. That's why I won't let you go." He trailed his mouth down, across her collarbone and below, to the swell of her breasts.

His dark hair brushed against her shoulder, her throat. She bit back a moan. "Ryder...please..." She arched her neck, curling her fingers around his shoulders.

He brought his face to hers, his breath whispering against her slightly parted lips. "You *think* you want him, but your body screams for me. Give in, Jen. Give in...."

He brought his mouth to hers. Open mouth to open mouth, tongue finding tongue. The meeting wasn't gentle, it wasn't nice. It was dark and desperate and wild; it was both of them needing beyond words or understanding.

She was on fire. Jennifer tightened her fingers, praying for sanity, holding on for dear life. She felt as if she were careening down a dark highway, the wind rushing past her, energizing her until she was aware of each nerve ending, every pore, until she understood the meaning of being totally and completely alive.

But with sensation came real fear. What waited at the end of the highway, the end of the ride, she could only guess at. She knew it would be wonderful, and she suspected it would change her, everything, forever.

Ryder moved his mouth from hers to the shell of her ear. She gulped in the cool night air. The oxygen, rather than steadying her, seemed to make her more light-headed. This was wrong, she told herself. It was dangerous. Anyone could come upon them. They would see and—

She couldn't stop him, she hadn't the will.

Jennifer arched her back, inviting him to sample whatever parts of her he wanted. He obliged, murmuring her name over and over almost reverently. Her hands strained at his back. She flexed her fingers and wished it was his muscled flesh beneath them instead of fabric, wished they were alone and naked.

Arousal—and fear—trembled through her. She'd never been with a boy—man—that way before, had never even imagined it. And now it felt as if she were already there.

Ryder pushed at the bodice of her dress. The night air stung her breasts and her nipples drew up into tight, protesting buds. Then his mouth was there, soothing and arousing, setting more fires.

Jennifer clutched him to her, terrified now that he would stop and she would never feel this way again.

But he didn't stop and then she understood he wouldn't. He was as aroused as she. It was there in the way his mouth moved almost greedily over her, in the impassioned way he murmured her name... but more in the way he, his hardness, pressed against her. She should be ashamed, she should be smart. All she knew was she wanted something that she couldn't put her finger on but burned inside her.

"Ryder..."

"Jen...oh, Jen..." He moved his mouth almost desperately over her. "What, baby? Tell me what you want."

"I don't know...." The breath shuddered past her lips. "Yes, I..."

"I know a place we can go—"

"Yes...no...Oh, Ryder..." She rested her forehead against his chest. "I'm so scared."

"Don't be scared, baby. I'll take care of you."

"But what if..." She moaned as he nipped her bottom lip, then tugged at her earlobe. "What if I got...you know? How would I face everyone? How could I explain this...us...."

Her words trailed off as she realized Ryder had become absolutely still. A second ticked by, then two. It seemed like an eternity to Jennifer. She rubbed her cheek against his satiny lapel, wishing for reassurance, wanting him to murmur that it would be all right, that he would take care of everything.

But he didn't. Instead Ryder dropped his hands and stepped away from her. Gone was the passionate boy of moments before, the boy who would have moved mountains to make her happy. Now the expression on his face was anything but warm or passionate.

Jennifer tugged her dress up over her breasts, feeling for the first time exposed and vulnerable.

"You're right, Jen. How could you explain?" He bit the words off so brutally it seemed as if he were spitting them at her. Then he turned and walked away.

Stunned, numb, Jennifer watched him go. He wouldn't be waiting for her inside, she knew. He might never be waiting for her again. Her legs began to shake and, wrapping her arms around herself, she sank onto a bench and cried.

Chapter Four

The rest of the prom passed in a blur, as did the beginning of the after-prom party. Drained, feeling betrayed, Jennifer stood at the edge of the gymnasium, smiling and waving to friends when she had to, hoping they wouldn't see how close to falling apart she was, hoping no one would ask about Ryder.

No one did. Her eyes pooled with tears once more, and she blinked against them. Everyone, it seemed, was having too good a time to pay much attention or be concerned with the way she felt or acted.

Thank goodness, her parents hadn't come. How would she have explained Ryder's absence to them? Jennifer clasped her hands in front of her. And how would she have kept from throwing herself into her father's arms and sobbing?

They'd been right to worry about Ryder after all.

Ryder. Biting her lip to keep from crying, Jennifer remembered the feel of his hands, his mouth on her breasts, remembered her own abandonment, and pain arced through her. Why had he been so cruel? And after he'd treated her so, how could she now want him to hold her and tell her everything was all right?

A single tear escaped and rolled down her cheek. She caught it quickly with her fingertip, blinking against others that trembled on her lashes. The things he'd said about her and her friends hurt just as badly. They'd been hateful, ugly.

"The three of you buzz around Sonny like bees looking for nectar..."

She tried to push the words—his words—out of her head. But they kept worming their way through, they kept eating at her.

"You call yourself friends—best friends—but the only thing you have in common is competition and keeping secrets, one secret in particular...."

It wasn't true! Jennifer shook her head and slipped through the crowd to the refreshment table. She collected an arm load of bowls and platters, then ducked into the equipment room to refill them. She sighed as the doors closed behind her, relieved to be away from the music and the sound of her classmates' laughter even if it was only for a moment.

Turning to the table laden with the snacks, she started to fill the plates.

"Hey, J.J."

Jennifer whirled around, hand to her throat. "Sonny, I didn't hear you come in."

"I know." He flashed her the smile that had melted the hearts of females six to sixty. Tonight it left Jennifer cold. He sauntered up to her, stopping close enough to touch.

She tipped her head back to meet his eyes. Yesterday she would have delighted in a moment like this with Sonny, tonight all she wanted was to be alone. "Where's Cyndi?"

"Around," he answered vaguely. "What's going on between you and Ryder?"

Her heart stopped. "What do you mean?"

"You guys disappeared and now Ryder's not here." He made a great show of looking around the storage room. "Or is he?"

She tightened her grip on the empty bowl in her hands. "No, he's not."

"Mmm." Sonny reached around her for a chip, his arm brushing her shoulder as he did. He smiled, and his dimple flashed. "So, what happened?"

Jennifer looked away. "Look, Sonny, I have to get these refreshments out. You can help if you want."

Sonny took the bowl from her but set it back on the table. He caught her hands and looked deeply into her eyes. It was the soul-searching gaze she'd been favored with on many previous occasions, but tonight there was something in his eyes that was out of control. Or maybe it was she who was out of control.

"J.J.," he said softly, coaxingly, "I need to talk to you. It's important."

Jennifer frowned. Something had upset him. He was trying to hide it, but it was there. But she was upset, too, and who did she have to go to? Who would listen to her? "Sonny, not now, I . . . this isn't a good ti—"

"You have to!" He squeezed her hands. "There's so much going on . . . I don't know what I'm going to do. Tonight Meredith—"

"Sonny—" she tugged against his grasp "—I'm really not up to this right now."

"But I need you, J.J. You can't turn me away." He lowered his voice to a husky drawl. "You can't."

She tugged her hands from his, angry with his attitude, sick to death of being Miss Congeniality. "Go talk to Cyndi, Sonny. *She's* your girlfriend. Not me."

"I can't talk to her, not the way I can talk to you." He put his hands on her shoulders and began moving his fingers in slow circles. "I'm going to break up with her, J.J. I know I didn't say anything before, but I felt sure you knew, that you sensed it. And I feel sure you know why."

"No." She shook her head and took a step back. He followed her. The table pressed against her hips.

"All these months," he said softly, "all the time we spent together . . . I know it meant as much to you as to me."

Ryder's words came back to her—words, in essence, about friendship and integrity. Could he have been right about her, about all of them? Repulsed by the thought, Jennifer flattened her hands against Sonny's chest and pushed him away. "Stop it, Sonny. Cyndi's my friend."

Sonny stared at her for a moment, his face blank with surprise. Then he narrowed his eyes. "What did

Hayes tell you? I can't believe I trusted that bastard!"

Jennifer swung away from him, afraid he would read everything she was thinking and feeling in her eyes. "Ryder has nothing to do with this. Cyndi's my friend and . . . and I want you to leave me alone."

Several seconds passed. Jennifer squeezed her eyes shut, waiting to hear the sound of the door closing behind him. It didn't come.

"I know, J.J."

Sonny's voice was normal again, deep and silky smooth. But it didn't charm her tonight, didn't make her feel bathed in that special Sonny light. Instead, a knot of apprehension settled in her stomach.

Stiffening her spine, she turned back to him. "Know what, Sonny?"

"About you and Ryder. He told me." He took a step closer to her. "You know, J.J., you could have picked a guy with a little more class. You could have picked me."

Jennifer's heart thundered in her chest, her palms grew damp. A part of her told herself not to ask, but the other part knew she had to. "What—" she cleared her throat "—did he tell you?"

"That you two were doing it."

She made some sound, of pain, of denial. She heard it even though it seemed to come from outside herself. She choked back another just like it. "No . . . he couldn't . . . wouldn't . . . surely you don't believe—"

"Don't try to deny it, J.J. I saw you tonight. I saw you two in the garden."

His words were like a blow to her chest; they took her breath, unbalanced her. She wrapped her arms around herself. "Get out of here, Sonny."

"Jennifer," he murmured coaxingly. Moving closer, he disentangled her arms and caught her hands in his. He rubbed them between his, warming them. "Let me stay. I don't care about Hayes. I forgive you." He drew her against his chest. "I love you. You have to know that."

She gazed up at his handsome face, shocked silent. Sonny loved her? Tomboy Jennifer, the girl with nothing more to commend her than being friendly?

Sonny smiled down at her, the curving of his lips confident to the point of arrogance. "I knew I could count on you, babe. I knew it." He lowered his head and caught her mouth.

Jennifer stood absolutely still as his mouth moved over hers. She'd waited for, had dreamed of this moment. But instead of delighting in his kiss, instead of feeling the wild heat she felt when Ryder touched her, she felt disgust—with him, with herself, with all of it.

Flattening her hands against his chest for the second time, she pushed. Surprised, he stumbled backward.

His blank expression would have been amusing in a different situation. It was obvious he hadn't thought her capable of refusing him, obvious he hadn't thought much at all.

Jennifer backed toward the door, her eyes filling once again. "Tonight, you'll have to find another shoulder," she said, her words more a croak than a whisper. "I suggest your girlfriend's."

Whirling around, she ran from the storage room, his stunned expression burned in her memory forever.

The next morning sunlight burned the back of her eyes. Her body ached. Her head throbbed. Jennifer groaned and tried to draw back into sleep.

"Jennifer...honey, wake up."

It was her father's voice, Jennifer realized, not her mother's. But her mother was there; she could smell her perfume and the scents of the kitchen that always seemed to follow her.

Something was wrong.

Jennifer opened her eyes, fear threading through her. At the expression on both her parents' faces, her heart began to pound. "What?" she asked, the sound raspy with sleep and apprehension.

"There's been an accident," her father said quietly. He sat on the edge of the bed, his hand on her arm. "Ryder's motorcycle—"

"Ryder! Oh, my God!" Jennifer shot up in bed, clutching her blanket to her chest. She fought to catch her breath, her world collapsing beneath her. "Is he hurt?" She grabbed at her father. "How bad—"

"Not Ryder, Jennifer. Sonny." Her father caught her hands and squeezed. "He's dead."

Chapter Five

Monday morning Jennifer pulled up in front of the Jennings and Joyce Real Estate office. Located on The Green in old downtown, the front window of their renovated storefront faced the statue of the town founder, Major A. W. Hazelhurst.

Sighing, Jennifer flipped down her sun visor and frowned into its tiny mirror. She didn't look good. In fact, she looked downright pale. Even her brilliant blue shirtwaist dress seemed lackluster and wilted today.

She frowned again. And she looked worried.

No wonder. Her mother and father had been tense and on edge all weekend. To make matters worse, the town was abuzz with the news that Ryder Hayes was back, and she'd been unable to avoid the questions, the speculation.

Hazelhurst was a small community with a small community's long memory and penchant for gossip. She shouldn't have been surprised that so many people remembered that she and Ryder used to see a lot of each other, but it had been a shock anyway.

Still staring into the mirror, Jennifer tried to relax her facial muscles, tried to smooth the tiny frown that formed between her brows. She'd halfway expected Ryder to try to contact her, had been sure that somehow, somewhere, she would have run into him.

She hadn't, but waiting for a ghost to pop up behind her had taken its toll, as had remembering the events of ten years ago. And, even though her weekend had passed at its usual breakneck pace, she'd done plenty of both.

Jennifer shook her head and snapped the visor back into place. But maybe, just maybe, the weekend was an indication of what was to come and Ryder wouldn't bother her.

After collecting her things, she stepped from the car. Nearly summer, the air was ripe with the scents of things that thrived in the heat, of new grass and blooming flowers. She smiled and breathed in its pungent sweetness, then started across the street.

Her partner's neat white BMW occupied the spot directly in front of their office, and Jennifer smiled and shook her head. Susan always arrived early—before the receptionist even—as if in defiance of the fact that Hazelhurst started its day with a putter rather than a burst.

Poor Susan. A crackerjack agent from Detroit who had consented to follow her physician husband to

Hazelhurst only on the condition he would finance her own agency, she made no secret of the fact she missed the big city's fast-paced real estate business and social scene.

"Morning, Sue," Jennifer called, juggling the door, her bulging briefcase and a cup of take-out coffee. Inside she dumped the briefcase onto the receptionist's desk, popped the lid off the coffee and sipped.

Susan came out of her office. "Thank God, you're here! Where do you keep your aspirin?"

"Patti keeps them for me. Top right drawer."

"Thanks." A moment later, Susan had downed several and perched on the edge of the desk, looking as tightly coiled as a snake. Jennifer studied her over the rim of her coffee cup. "Good weekend?"

Susan groaned and pushed her fingers through her short, sable-brown bob. "The dinner party was a disaster and Bill's new associate and his wife are deadly boring. I thought I would go out of my mind when she started talking about her son's potty training."

Jennifer bit back a laugh. Although she and Susan were too different to ever really be friends, they got along and worked well together. She supposed it was their differences that made both possible. "Sounds like a mess."

"Funny." Susan took a cigarette from her gold monogrammed case and lit it. "How was yours?"

"My Little Leaguers won."

Susan pulled on the cigarette than blew out the smoke in a long, slow stream. "Big excitement."

Jennifer smiled at the sarcasm in the other woman's voice. "It was. They went to extra innings."

"Do we have anything going on this week?"

She and Susan had worked together for over a year, but her partner's lightning-fast change of subjects still took her by surprise anyway. "Pardon?"

Susan took another drag on the cigarette, then snubbed it out. Standing, she began to pace. "Business sucks."

Jennifer sipped her coffee, watching the other woman move back and forth across the office, the frustration emanating from her almost palpable. Jennifer knew her behavior had more to do with ambition and boredom than real financial concerns.

"I have seen better," Jennifer said. "But remember, the schools let out next week, and a lot of people wait until then to make a move."

"Don't sugarcoat it for me, Jennifer. We both know the economy around here is as stagnant as a dead lake."

And it could get worse. Jennifer thought of Ryder, her father and the plant closing, and she suppressed a shudder. *It wasn't going to happen. It couldn't.*

"There's nothing we can do about the economy, Susan," she said carefully. "We've got several sales pending and some of the most desirable properties in Hazelhurst listed with us." Jennifer shrugged. "I think, considering the circumstances, that we're doing well."

Susan stopped pacing and glared at her. "You're such an annoying little optimist."

Jennifer laughed. "You say that as if you'd like to strangle me."

"Cheerfully." Susan laughed then, too. "Okay, so I'm a tad intense."

"A tad?"

"I'm entitled." Susan sniffed and returned to her original position on the edge of the desk and lit another cigarette. "Speaking of intense, you really tore out of here Friday afternoon."

Jennifer's smile faded. "I had something on my mind."

"I gathered that much. Anything you want to share?"

"No." She smiled brightly. "But thanks anyway."

"Suit yourself."

Jennifer heard the question in her partner's voice, the question and the hint of something else—hurt maybe—and feeling disappointed with herself, stood and collected her briefcase. Why couldn't she just open up and tell Susan what was going on? Why, when she even thought about doing so, did a knot form in her chest? "I guess it's time to get to it. Anything else I should know about?"

"Yeah, you have a new client." Susan put out her cigarette. "He stopped in late Friday, after you left. He's coming in around two to discuss his needs."

"Is he looking to buy?"

"Lease. But for the right property, he'll consider a lease-purchase. He said he was an old friend of yours."

"An old friend," Jennifer repeated, a trickle of apprehension stealing up her spine. It couldn't be...he wouldn't. She'd lived in Hazelhurst all her life, she had many friends, many acquaintances. She—

"Hayes is his name. Ryder Hayes."

The overloaded briefcase slipped from her fingers, her composure with it. *Ryder had contacted her, she just hadn't known it.*

"Are you all right?"

Jennifer met her partner's concerned—and surprised—gaze. "Yes," she managed, stooping to collect the case, using the time to collect herself, as well. Straightening, she expelled a long, slow breath. "I can't work with him, Susan. Sorry."

The other woman lifted an eyebrow. "Maybe we both had better sit down and discuss this."

"There's nothing to discuss."

"Who is this guy, an old lover or something?"

Or something. What an appropriate description for what their relationship had been. Jennifer sank into a chair. "No," she murmured after a moment. "We were friends. We were all friends back then."

Again a single sable brow arched. "Then what's this all about?"

Susan deserved an answer. They were partners and this was business. But just as she'd been unable to confide her deepest feelings to Cyndi and Meredith ten years ago, she couldn't share them now.

"You wouldn't understand, Susan," she said finally. "You're not from around here."

"Which is precisely why I took you on. You know everyone. They come to you when they want to buy, when they want to list their home. This town is like an exclusive club, a club for which I don't have a membership card. You do, Jennifer. I offered you a percentage of my business because of that in. You owe me an explanation.''

''You work with him. I give him to you.''

''We both know that's not the way it works. Besides, he wants you. He was quite specific on that point, Jennifer—it's you or the competition.''

Jennifer stood and crossed to the window. Outside, three high-school-age girls stood talking to a boy in a red convertible. She thought again of her old friends. What had happened to them? Had they thought of her as often in the past ten years as she'd thought of them? Had their futures also been skewed by the events of ten years ago?

''Does this have something to do with Sonny Keighton?''

The question stole her carefully crafted calm, and Jennifer whirled around. ''What?''

''I wasn't in town a week before I learned about this paragon. 'Sonny Keighton took Hazelhurst High to the state championships two years in a row. A feat,''' Susan mimicked, '' 'that hadn't been done before and hasn't since.' '' She shuddered elegantly. ''God, I hate sports. And jocks. Why people worship them is beyond me.''

''People need heroes,'' Jennifer said softly. ''But it was more than his football record that made Sonny special.''

''Then this does have something to do with him.''

Jennifer nodded and lowered her eyes to her hands. ''He was killed the night of the senior prom. He was driving Ryder Hayes's motorcycle.'' A motorcycle that should have been parked in his driveway, she thought.

A motorcycle he'd promised he wouldn't drive that night. "They'd both been drinking."

"You were kids," Susan said softly. "Kids do crazy things...sometimes they get hurt. Tragic, but..." She let her words trail off.

That sounded so simple, Jennifer thought. But it hadn't been, wasn't. Still she felt so many things she couldn't explain, wouldn't even if she could. Things like anger, like guilt and betrayal.

Susan drained her coffee and stood. "Look, I'm sorry there's bad blood between you and this guy, but the fact is he wants to work with you. The national chains have been kicking our butt and with the economy what it is, nobody's buying. I want you to take this client—who knows—maybe he wants to make peace."

Jennifer met Susan's eyes. "Is that an order?"

She sighed. "No, Jennifer. But I want you to give this a lot of thought. You know where I—the agency—stands on this."

Give it thought? Jennifer almost laughed out loud. In truth she would probably do nothing but think about it. And Sonny. And the night that had changed her life forever.

Susan checked her watch. "Patti's going to be late again." She reached for the phone to call their flighty receptionist. As she dialed the number, she looked back up at Jennifer. "And while you're thinking, consider this—you're on your own here. If you don't want to work with him, you tell him."

"Fair enough," Jennifer murmured. Without another word, she picked up her briefcase and went into her office.

Ryder arrived at two twenty-three. Jennifer knew the exact moment he walked into the office. It could have been her imagination or hearing him speak, but irrationally it seemed as if she felt his presence.

Ridiculous! Jennifer shook herself. She was on edge, sensitized because she'd spent too much time the past few days dredging up old memories, old hurts. It was time to get a grip.

All her bravado proved just that when she saw him. He was talking to Susan, smiling at her in that wicked way of his. Patti was hanging on every word like a besotted puppy.

Denying the way her own heart thundered against the wall of her chest, she trailed her gaze over him. He wore jeans again, coal black this time and brand-new looking save for creases she had no business noticing. His thick, dark hair fell slightly across his forehead, his white oxford-cloth shirt was open at the collar.

When she realized she was staring at the small triangle of flesh exposed by that open button, she jerked her gaze away.

And then she noticed the motorcycle helmet dangling loosely from his left hand.

Her blood went cold. Why had she expected him to have been affected by the past? The Ryder she'd known had never given a damn about anything but defiance.

"Ryder."

The trio looked at her, the two women obviously surprised by the sharpness of her tone. She ignored them both, focusing on him. "Susan said I should expect you."

"Jen."

Soft as silk, smooth as brandy, his voice, like his face, gave nothing away. Nothing but the absolute maleness of him. Patti nearly swooned; Susan grinned. Jennifer motioned her office door. "Come in."

Once inside, Jennifer closed the door behind them and faced him. "I'm not amused by this stunt."

Ryder slipped his hands into the front pockets of his jeans. "Stunt?"

"Let's not waste our time. Considering the circumstances, I don't think it's wise that we work together."

"Really?" He arched his eyebrows in innocent surprise. Her blood pressure went up several notches. "What circumstances are those?"

She folded her arms across her chest. "Don't play dumb, Ryder. It doesn't become you."

"And evasion doesn't become you. Spit it out, Jen."

"Fine. For starters, your position at the plant. You hold my father's future in the palm of your hand."

"It would seem to me," he murmured, lowering his voice to a husky drawl, "that you might want to be extra nice for just that reason."

His inference was clear and she swung away from him, furious. "You make me sick."

He caught her arm and swung her back around. "Do I?"

"Yes." She narrowed her eyes. "Take your hand off me."

Instead of doing as she asked, he moved it until his fingers circled her wrist. "What other reasons, Jen?"

She inched her chin up. "Our past."

"So, now you admit we have one."

"I never denied that, Ryder."

"Oh, that's right. You only denied what you felt every time I touched you." He dragged his thumb across her wrist. "Do you still feel it?"

Jennifer tugged against his grasp, hoping he didn't feel the unsteadiness of her pulse but knowing he couldn't miss the wild color in her cheeks. "Leave. Now."

He laughed coolly, almost arrogantly. "The Jennifer I thought I knew wouldn't have turned away a friend in need."

Pain and guilt speared through her. *Sonny.* She'd turned him away and he'd died. "You didn't know me very well."

He tightened his fingers for a moment then released her. "That became obvious ten years ago."

"You act like you were the one hurt. You act like I should apologize to you."

"Do I?"

His blue eyes burned with something deeply felt, fierce even. Jennifer fought against the emotions that stirred inside of her. Tipping her chin up, she held his gaze. "Yes. And I can't imagine why."

"That's what's so pathetic," he murmured so softly she had to strain to hear. He turned away from her. "Do you remember the day the five of us ditched school and went out to Crystal Lake for a picnic?"

Jennifer folded her arms across her chest. She didn't want to remember; she wished she couldn't. Ryder had kissed her for the first time. "Yes."

"That day was a revelation to me. I remember feeling that life had possibilities, that there were options for me." He met her eyes. "It was the first time I realized I didn't have to become my father."

Pain, as sweet as it was debilitating, ballooned inside her. She struggled against the sensation just as she struggled to control the runaway beat of her heart. In that moment she was eighteen again and breathlessly awaiting her own future.

He closed the distance between them. "Even as young and stupid as I'd been then, I'd been right. Not about all my...possibilities. But some." He cupped her cheek in his palm. "You say you feel nothing for me."

Her breath caught. "I don't."

He moved his hand so his fingers tangled in her hair. "Nothing at all?"

"Anger," she whispered, cursing the huskiness of her voice. "Disgust that you could stoop so low as to seek revenge like this."

He laughed. The sound was soft and male, dangerous because of its effect on her. "If that's all, why are you afraid of working with me?"

"I'm not." She wetted her lips. "It's a matter of principle. It's—"

"That you don't trust yourself with me."

"Not true." Even as the words passed her lips, she knew she was a liar. She suspected he knew it, too.

"Prove it, J.J."

Furious, she stepped back, away from his touch. He didn't resist. That truth had heat stinging her cheeks once more. "Okay, Ryder, I could use the commission. You've got yourself an agent. But don't expect the obliging, naive girl you knew ten years ago."

The sound he made was hard. His expression was more so. "I don't have that much imagination, Jen. Not anymore."

Chapter Six

This wasn't supposed to have happened. Ryder dragged his hands through his hair and stared out the one window in the office he still shared with Henry Joyce. Dammit, he wasn't supposed to feel anything for her.

He'd been certain he could make this trip down memory lane without a hitch. The final test for himself, proof positive that he'd left Hazelhurst and the events of his past behind.

But here he stood, tied into a dozen different knots and aching over the same woman he'd assured himself he'd forgotten long ago.

He'd flunked his own test.

Ryder whirled away from the window. How could he have known there would be ghosts in her eyes? And even if he had known, he never would have guessed how those shadows would pull at him. Or make him push at her.

Leave it alone, man. Cut and run.

Ryder turned back to the window, back to the brilliant day. Jennifer had betrayed him. She'd broken his heart. If she had ghosts, they were her problem. He had his own to contend with.

Frowning, he pressed his palms against the window frame, squinting against the light that streamed through the panes of glass. It wasn't a day for ghosts, not a day for memories that clawed at him.

But here they were anyway, dredged up by a wisp of a woman with auburn hair and a smile that didn't quite reach her eyes.

Ryder closed his own eyes. He thought back ten years, to the morning he had awakened to the news that he'd killed his best friend.

The first thing he'd been aware of had been pain. Stunning, unbelievably intense, it had throbbed through him until even his vision blurred. Although his entire body had ached, the pain had been most excruciating in his head and middle. Breathing had been agony, thinking an exercise in terror.

He hadn't known, not at first, where he was or why. There'd been no loving family waiting by the bed, no worried friends. Only the nurses, their attitudes ranging from curt to kind, had come and gone from his room. One had finally and none too gently reminded him of the accident.

And that Sonny was dead.

Memory of the accident had come barreling back in kaleidoscope fashion, a jumble of colors and sounds and thoughts. There had been Sonny, his mood dark, terrifying in its mercurial intensity. There had been the roar of the bike's engine, the wind screaming past his ears. Sonny's wild laughter as he took each corner faster, the headlight as it sliced across the bleak stretch of road. Then there had been a brick wall rising up to meet them and the moment he realized they were going to crash, that he was going to die.

But he hadn't died.

Sonny. Ryder stared up at the antiseptic white ceiling. He should feel grief, despair or even a secret relief to be alive. Instead his feelings were a frightening mix of all of those.

Plus anger. At Sonny for throwing away their friendship, with thinking so little of their lives to be so reckless with them.

Ryder fought them all, staring up at the ceiling, focusing instead on his physical pain and the hope that Jennifer would come to see him.

His mother came, finally, and cowered by the bed as if afraid to be discovered there. Ryder knew then that his father had forbidden her to visit. He smiled at her, trying to be strong, assuring her his bruises were nothing, that he would be his old self in a matter of minutes. For sure.

After all, how could he tell her, his mother, that he would never be his old self again?

His father came next. He reeked of whiskey. His eyes were dark with fury, cold from years of hard drinking and even harder knocks. Too weak to fight back or run, Ryder gazed up at him. All the times in the past months he'd interceded for his brothers and sisters, all the times he'd stood, fists clenched and ready beside his mother, flashed like obscene photographs on the back of his eyes.

With those pictures came fear, stronger, more potent even than the moment he'd realized Sonny was dangerously drunk and totally out of control. And for the first time since puberty he wondered if, this time, his father would kill him.

"So this is what your fancy girl and fancy friends bring you," his father said, his voice thick with drink. "Puttin' on airs and rentin' tuxedos, thinkin' you're better than where you come from ... better than your old man."

His father curled his hands into fists, and Ryder looked frantically at the doorway. When no one magically appeared, he reached for the nurses' call button.

"All these gadgets cost money!" His father waved his hand at the monitor by the bed and the IV drip, his voice raising. "Who's gonna pay for all this? You think old man Joyce is goin' to keep me on now?" He looked back at Ryder, the coldness in his eyes replaced by a heat Ryder recognized too well. "Answer me, boy! Did you think of that when you were off gettin' your fancy butt tore up?"

Ryder found the button and closed his fingers around the cool, smooth plastic.

"I should have yanked you out of that school long ago and put you to work!" his father raged. "You can go up to the plant and support me...how would ya like that, boy? No-good kid, I'll teach you to forget where you come from!"

His father raised his hand, and Ryder stared up at him, fighting the urge to cringe back against the pillows or call out. He'd promised himself he would never again give his old man that satisfaction.

"Mr. Hayes! What do you think you're doing?"

His father wheeled around at the nurse's outraged voice, nearly stumbling. "Nothin'," he muttered, trying to regain his balance. "Just kissin' my boy goodbye, that's all."

"Well, I think you had better leave." The nurse marched across to the bed. "Now, please."

His father looked back at him, and for a moment Ryder thought he actually *was* going to kiss him. His stomach rose to his throat, then without another word, his father turned and walked away.

Ryder shifted his gaze from the now-empty doorway to the woman hovering beside him. She was one of the kind nurses, one of the ones who had talked softly to him each time she'd come through.

And now she knew.

Embarrassment welled inside him and stung his cheeks until he felt about six years old and totally ridiculous. He lowered his eyes, not wanting to see the look in hers—her sympathy, her distaste.

"There you go," she murmured, straightening his blankets, plumping his pillows. "Nice and comfy. Can I get you anything?"

Ryder took a deep, painful breath. "I don't want him in here," he whispered, hearing, to his horror, the way tears choked the words.

"I'll see to it." She plumped his pillow again, then touched his forehead, just once and lightly. "You'd better sleep now."

He did. And when he awoke, Jen was there. She stood by the doorway as if ready for flight, her face pale, her expression stricken.

She'd come.

The relief he'd expected earlier, flowed through him now, clean and sweet and warming. In that moment, every one of his pains eased and the ugliness of his father's visit evaporated. It was as if with her had come light and the promise of a new day.

Ryder tried to say her name, to smile, but couldn't. Emotion clogged his throat, stole his breath. He ached to hold her, for her to hold him. He wished he could make her pain go away.

He could do none of those things, so he gazed at her instead, letting everything he felt shine from his eyes.

If she read his silent messages, if she understood, she gave no indication of it. She hovered there, just inside the door, not making a move to come closer. Seconds ticked past, and as each one did, his chest tightened with apprehension.

"Sonny's dead," she whispered finally. "Did you know that?"

He nodded, his eyes, like hers, filling with tears.

"I should have known better," she continued, clasping her hands in front of her. "I've been so stupid. So naive." Her voice broke, her tears spilled over.

"Jenni... fer... Jen, don't cry. I—"

"No." She shook her head, swiping at the tears on her cheeks. "Everyone tried to warn me, my parents, friends, teachers. But I wouldn't listen. I thought I knew you, thought they were being unfair...because of your father—''

She covered her face with her hands for a moment, the sound of her grief an agony for him. When she looked at him again, her eyes were once more dry. But the emotion that burned in them had his heart thumping against the wall of his chest.

''I trusted you,'' she said evenly. ''You lied. About me. To Sonny. I was your friend...your—''

Her voice caught, the sound tore at him. A split second later, the meaning of her words became clear— she blamed him for Sonny.

Just as his father did, just as the nurses, the doctors, the cop who had taken his statement.

No wonder no one had come to see him. He had taken their hero away. He was a defiler and a murderer.

And now, the one person he'd thought believed in him—the person he had relied on believing in him— stood accusing without trial, without questions.

The pain was back, worse now, ripping and tearing at him. And in that moment he wanted to die, wished he had been the one thrown into the brick wall instead of away from it.

But no one would have blamed Sonny even though he'd been driving the bike. They would have clucked their tongues and shaken their heads. ''Poor boy,'' they would have said. ''We knew something like this would happen some day.''

And life in Hazelhurst would have gone on with barely a pause or tear shed.

Anger assuaged the pain, if only a bit. He wouldn't defend himself, was done defending himself—to his father, this town, to Jennifer.

He looked at her, stripping his expression of everything but the anger. And the defiance.

She took a step backward, a sob wrenching from her throat. Several moments passed, she opened her mouth as if to speak, then turned and ran from the room.

After she left, he'd cried. In a way he hadn't since he was a small boy, in a way he promised himself he never would again. Then, when he'd felt stronger, after they had given him his pain medication, he'd gotten up and checked himself out of the hospital. Then out of Hazelhurst.

Forever, he'd thought.

Ryder opened his eyes to the spring day that was so much like the one he'd stepped out into ten years before. He shouldn't have come back, should have refused this assignment. He knew that now. Now that it was too late.

Ryder turned away from the day. Gracing Henry Joyce's desk were several pictures of Jennifer. He crossed to the desk and picked up the first, one of Jennifer the way he remembered her—eighteen, full of laughter and love of life. She'd posed for the picture in her cheerleader's uniform, standing on the field, the sun streaming over her, turning her hair to fire. His gut twisted just a little, and he set it down and reached for another.

This one was recent, obviously a studio shot, its mood more somber. In it, lovely, grown-up Jennifer smiled at the camera with the same aloofness he sensed in her, the same ghosts lurking behind her eyes. He touched the surface of the glass lightly with his index finger, then realized what he was doing, swore and set it back down.

He turned toward his own, smaller desk, the one Henry Joyce had shoved into a corner for him. No pictures graced its top. Instead the desk was littered with productivity reports, cost outlays and printouts containing information about every facet of the plant's operation and how much that facet made or cost the corporation.

Ryder took one last look at the photos, then settled himself behind his desk. As he did, the office door opened and Henry Joyce strode through, his expression murderous.

"Hayes."

Ryder smiled at Henry's use of his last name. The man meant to show disrespect; Ryder preferred knowing exactly where he stood. "Henry, good to see you."

"Cut the nicey-nice crap, Hayes." He stopped in front of Ryder's desk, fists on his hips. "We need to talk."

"My office is yours," Ryder murmured, loosening his tie, then easing back in his chair. Henry Joyce's already flushed features reddened more.

"I hear you were out in the shop this morning."

Ryder inclined his head.

"Looks to me like you have plenty to keep you busy right here."

"What's your point?"

Henry placed his hands on the desk and leaned toward him. "I don't want you out there talking to the men. They have jobs to do, quotas to make. They don't need a distraction."

Henry Joyce wasn't a tall man, but big and barrel chested, with a strong jaw and booming voice. He cut an intimidating figure. Ryder was neither impressed nor intimidated. He eased forward until he and Henry were nose to nose. "This process would be a lot easier if you'd swallow your righteous indignation and cooperate."

Henry made a sound of disgusted disbelief. "Why would I want to make it easier for you?"

"Not me." Ryder stood, forcing the other man to straighten if he still wanted to look him in the eye. "I don't have a problem with the job I do. I'm used to being disliked. Used to walls. And I'm here, and am staying until the job's done. So, make *your* life a little easier, Henry, and quit with the attitude." He held out his hand. "What do you say?"

"Go to hell."

Ryder shrugged and slipped his hands into his pockets. He hadn't expected anything different. He kept his gaze fixed on the other man's. "Is that all you wanted?"

Henry paused, obviously curious about what he'd been talking to the guys in the shop about but unwilling to give even a fraction of an inch. Ryder understood the game and the other man's need for a sense of power, of control. He let him off the hook. "Your spies were right, Henry. I spent the morning in the shop talking to the guys. I wanted to find out if they were happy and why or why not."

"Happy!" The word exploded from the older man. "What does it matter? They're here to do a job. They're paid well to do it. Not to chitchat with some boy intent on putting them on the unemployment line. Not to whine about whether they're happy or not."

"You're so sure I'm going to shut you down?" Ryder asked, his voice soft with control. Everyone in this town had always been so sure of everything he did—so sure without ever looking at the evidence, without asking a simple question.

Henry looked at him intently. "Can you honestly say it wouldn't be sweet revenge? A way to punish this town for your old man? To punish me for the stand I took as Jennifer's father?"

It was between them now—his father, his relationship with Jennifer. Ryder met the other man's steely gaze with his own. "There are many forms of revenge," he murmured. "Many ways to settle scores."

Henry swore. "That's it, isn't it? The paperwork's not good enough to hang us on, so you're going to use the men's dissatisfaction to seal our fate."

Ryder laughed, the sound hard even to his own ears. "You can't imagine why I would want to talk to the guys at the machines. You can't conceive that what's going on with them might really matter, or that they might be a key ingredient in turning productivity around."

"They make a damn good wage—the union sees to that. What more do they want?"

"The happier the worker, the more productive."

This time it was Henry who laughed. "That's college classroom bull and training seminar crapola. Don't tell me how to get a full day's work out of the men. Twenty years ago I came into *this plant* and turned it around. Me." He thumped himself on the chest. "For twenty years there hasn't been a problem, this plant has made money for the corporation and supported the people of Hazelhurst."

"That's right, Henry. Twenty years ago you came in, kicked butt and took names."

"Damn right. And it worked."

"Yeah, it worked. *Twenty years ago.* Those hard-ball management techniques don't cut it anymore. Take a look, there are your figures." Ryder picked up a couple of files and shoved them across the desk. "The workers of the nineties aren't sheep. They don't scare into performing. And they want respect. They want incentives and pats on the back for a job well-done. They want to feel like they're more than strong backs on a time clock. They want to feel like they make a difference."

"I've heard all this 'team' concept stuff before. But I've never seen it work." Henry threw up his hands. "What are you going to suggest next? Substance-abuse programs and flex-time? Maybe we should even get an interior decorator in to make the shop more livable?"

"Yeah, how about those?" Ryder shot back, angry at the sarcasm in the other man's voice. Maybe if somebody had offered his father a way out, an ultimatum that was paid for, instead of threats and looking the other way, maybe he wouldn't have died a miserable drunk. "Those are good ideas. Ideas that have been proven to work."

Henry laughed without humor. "We'll be out of business for sure. Who's going to pay for them? The corporation? That's a laugh. We have to fight to keep toilet paper in the johns." Henry started for the door. "Fairy tales, Hayes."

"At least fairy tales offer happy endings. Your way, ambivalence and status quo, doesn't offer anyone anything worthwhile." Ryder stood, holding on to his temper but not tightly enough to keep it from spilling over into his words. "I heard Mac McPherson's wife just had a baby. I also heard you denied him a week's leave to help out."

Henry stopped but didn't turn. "He'd used all his time."

"Sometimes exceptions have to be made."

"I didn't think so."

Ryder swore at his own inability to remain impartial, at Henry Joyce's hardheadedness. "How often do you take a stroll out into the shop to see how the guys are doing...to ask how their families are or just shoot the breeze for a minute?"

Henry wheeled around. "You think you can do better? Here." He tossed his plant keys at Ryder. "Take 'em. Save us both the aggravation."

Ryder caught the keys, then held them back out to the older man. "Keep them. This thing's far from sorted out."

Henry folded his arms across his chest. They faced each other, moments passed. Still Ryder held the keys out. Henry Joyce didn't budge, and Ryder knew he wouldn't. His had been a heroic gesture, an act of pride. Henry Joyce would never take them back of his own accord.

Ryder tossed the keys to the other man. "I insist, Joyce."

Henry caught them, and Ryder couldn't help noticing the possessive way his fingers curled around them as he did. In that moment he understood how much it had taken for the man to throw them away and just how much this job meant to him.

Ryder scowled. He didn't want to know. He couldn't afford to give a damn.

Just as he couldn't afford to wonder about the ghosts in Jennifer's eyes.

The intercom buzzed. Both men made a move for it, but Ryder was closer. "Yes, Dottie?"

"Jennifer...Joyce is here."

"Tell her to wait," Henry boomed from behind him. "Tell her I'll be out in a moment."

Ryder turned back to the other man, arching an eyebrow at the expression on his face. It was the same one he'd been subjected to every time he had picked Jennifer up for a date. "Is there something else you want to say to me?"

"Stay away from my daughter."

"I think that decision's out of your hands."

"Keep your hands and everything else away from Jennifer. Or I'll—"

"You'll what?" Ryder tightened his jaw. "She's not eighteen anymore. Neither am I."

"Don't push me, Hayes."

"And don't *you* push me. Your daughter's waiting." Ryder turned back to his desk, dismissing the other man, ending the conversation. He heard Henry release an angry breath, then open the door.

"Jennifer, honey, what a nice surprise."

Ryder picked up a file, determined to ignore them both.

"Dad, hi." Jennifer kissed her father's cheek, her eyes going almost unwittingly to Ryder's back as she did. She drew away then, searching her father's expression. In her own expression, she knew, he would read concern. She couldn't help herself. "Everything's okay?"

"Fine, baby. Just fine."

She frowned and looked at Ryder again. "I didn't think you would still be sharing your office."

"His will be ready by the end of the week. Now, to what do I owe the pleasure of this visit?"

Not what. Who. "Well..." She drew the word out, knowing how what she had to say was going to sound and how her father was going to take it. She decided to just spit it out. "I came to speak with Ryder."

"I see."

Dammit. She caught his hand. "But we'll talk later. I thought maybe we could go out for a drink." She squeezed his fingers. "Okay?"

"Fine." He shot Ryder an icy stare. Jennifer saw then that Ryder had turned around and was watching them with amusement. "I've got some things to do."

"I'll find you when I'm done here," she murmured, and caught his hand. "I love you."

He smiled a little, then left the office.

When the door clicked shut behind him, she turned and faced Ryder. ''You are such a bastard.''

He pushed away from his desk and crossed to her. ''Am I?''

''Yes.'' She tipped her chin up. ''What were you talking about before I arrived? You upset him.''

''My being here upsets him.'' Ryder reached out and touched her cheek. It was like silk under his finger. ''Among other things, he told me to stay away from you.''

She swore. ''How am I going to explain this?''

''Same old story, Jennifer.'' Ryder narrowed his eyes. ''Seems to me the truth might work.''

''The truth?'' Jennifer repeated, an odd ache in her chest.

''You came to show me some properties. Right?''

''Right,'' Jennifer repeated, taking the easy way out, feeling like a fraud. Yes, she had come with properties to show him. But she could have described them over the phone. They both knew that. Her father would, also.

The truth was, the properties had been an excuse. She'd been unable to stop thinking of him since their meeting that afternoon, and although she wasn't sure why it had seemed so urgent to see him, and even though she'd tried to talk herself out of it, she had come.

Now she was here. And she felt like a total idiot.

She indicated her briefcase. ''I have some properties I think you'll be inter—''

''Fine.''

''Shall I describe—''

"No. I'll look at them all."

"All right." She caught her bottom lip between her teeth. "Is tomorrow good for you?"

"Better make it the day after." Ryder slipped his hands into his pockets to keep from touching her again. "Late afternoon—say three?"

"Shall I meet you here?"

"No, I'll meet you at your office."

"Okay." She searched for something else to say, some reason that she should stay a few more minutes. That there was no good reason made her feel even more ridiculous. She started for the door, stopping when she had her hand on the knob. "I'll see you Wednesday afternoon then."

"Jen?" She met his eyes. "One question about the properties—is Sonny's parents' house among them?"

Jennifer stared at him, stunned. "What?"

"I understand it's up for lease."

It took a moment for his words to register. When they did, anger replaced shock. Her heart began to pound against her chest. "They would never lease to you."

"They would have to. There are such things as antidiscrimination laws. But you know that."

"I don't think—"

"I want you to show it to me."

"No." She shook her head. "I can't."

He crossed to her and caught her hands, lacing their fingers. "I need to see it, Jen."

Jennifer searched his expression. Something in his eyes ached. Something there assured her that this wasn't about revenge, that it was about healing instead of hurting.

Understanding, unwanted, curled through her. And with it came softness, as unexpected as it was unsolicited. It stole over her until her knees were weak and her head light.

She lowered her eyes to their joined hands. His were harder than hers, stronger. His flesh was darker, toughened from years of physical labor.

But now he worked behind a desk. She drew her eyebrows together even as she moved her thumb ever so slightly across his. There was a rightness about his touching her... a completeness.

There always had been.

Her breath caught at the truth of that and at the awareness that came with it. No. It couldn't be. She wouldn't allow it to be. She began to ease her hand from his.

He tightened his fingers. "Come have a drink with me."

"My father," she murmured.

"Cancel."

"No." She shook her head, shocked that she wanted to go—badly. She tugged her hand from his. "I can't."

"Or won't?"

"Same thing."

She reached for the doorknob, and he stopped her once more. "What about the Keighton place, Jen?"

"I don't know," she said softly, looking back at him. "I'll think about it, but I can't guarantee—"

He caught her words with his mouth. Surprised, her head fell back and her lips parted. His brushed against hers, feather light and for only a moment. She thought she might faint anyway. She wrapped the fingers of her free hand around his shoulder to steady herself.

"Didn't anyone ever tell you, Jen?" he whispered, drawing away from her. "There are no guarantees." He touched her mouth with his forefinger, then took a step back. "'Maybe' will just have to be good enough."

Not knowing what to say, Jennifer turned and fled from the office.

Her father was waiting for her. She forced herself to meet his eyes and smile brightly. She hoped he wouldn't see or sense how torn she was.

He returned her smile, but the curving of his lips was as tense as the rest of him seemed to be. The expression in his eyes was...hurt. Jennifer's heart turned over. He'd always been there for her, always been her hero. He needed her now—her support and understanding, her loyalty. She couldn't forget that.

But neither could she seem to forget the brush of Ryder's mouth against her own. The imprint of his lips still burned on hers.

"I hope I'm not taking you away from anything important," she said, stopping beside him.

He laid an arm across her shoulders. "Nothing's more important than my baby girl."

Guilt curled through her. "Where would you like to go? Clancy's?"

He thought that was fine, and they headed across the street to the Irish pub-style bar. After they'd seated themselves across from each other in the kelly-green booths and ordered their drinks, her father cleared his throat. "This is nice."

She shifted in her seat. "Yes."

"We don't get to do it enough." He paused. "I'm glad you . . . stopped by."

Jennifer knew what he was getting at. Considering the circumstances, she didn't blame him for wanting to know. "Ryder's hired me—the agency—to help him find a house to lease. I brought him information on . . . a few properties—" she stopped talking as the waitress served their drinks, continuing when she'd left again "—I'd like to show him. We're meeting day after tomorrow."

"I see."

The guilt of before doubled. Hating herself for it and the need she felt to justify herself, she went on. "You know, business has been bad. Susan's concerned. Even one lease . . . is . . . important."

"If the plant closes," her father murmured, "Susan might as well pack it up and return to Detroit."

Everything always came back to Ryder. Jennifer caught her bottom lip between her teeth. "The other day you seemed more optimistic. You seemed to think this would all blow over—"

"That was the other day." Henry clinked his ice against the side of his glass for a moment, then took a sip of the drink. "And your mother was there." He drew his eyebrows together. "I'm worried about her."

"Mom?" Concerned, Jennifer leaned forward in her seat.

Her father looked past her for a moment. "When you and Christopher were kids, I purposefully didn't talk about problems. Kids shouldn't have to worry, there's enough time for that when they grow up." He smiled at her again, this time with more than a trace of wistfulness. "You're all grown-up now, Jennifer."

She reached across the table and caught his big hand. He curled his fingers around hers. "I like to think so."

"I know I forget that sometimes...a father's right, I like to think." He took another sip of the cocktail. "Your mother's so settled. She has her friends and her clubs."

"Her garden."

"Right." He laughed a little and shook his head. "I'm worried about a move, worried she won't be happy anywhere but Hazelhurst."

Jennifer sat up straighter. "A move? Has something happened that I haven't heard—"

"No, nothing's happened." He squeezed her fingers reassuringly. "But this thing at the plant doesn't look good. I just don't trust that boy to be fair." Henry searched her expression. "What do you think, Jenny?"

Surprised by both the question and his childhood pet name for her, she groped for a response. "Well, I...he..."

She let her words trail off. The truth was, she didn't know what to think. On a gut level she couldn't believe he would deliberately hurt her or Hazelhurst, but on every other level she could see how bad it looked.

Her father squeezed her fingers, then withdrew his hand. "I imagine this is difficult for you. But I have to tell you what I think. And I think that boy has a chip on his shoulder the size of Plymouth Rock. Now, I can't say I blame him and I can see where he might mistakenly hold me responsible for some of his woes, but that doesn't change the facts any. I'm afraid his mind is made up."

Ryder. Jennifer thought of the look in his eyes when he'd asked to go to Sonny's house, remembered the way his mouth had felt against hers, and her chest ached. She opened her mouth to defend Ryder but closed it again. What could she say? Ryder had every reason to want revenge, and he was in a perfect position to get it.

Her father reached across the table and caught her hands. "You are all grown-up, but I can't help worrying about you, can't seem to take my own advice to butt out and mind my own business."

Jennifer stiffened, suspecting what would come next. "Dad—"

"He's not the boy for you, Jenny. He never has been."

Hurt, she withdrew her hands from his. "Do you think there's something going on between me and Ryder?"

"I didn't say that. It's just that in high school you two were close and now he's back. I'm just worried..."

His voice trailed off and silence enveloped them for several moments, then he sighed again. "I only want

the best for you, Jennifer. You've always been...
special to me."

Tears sprang to her eyes. She blinked against them.
"I hope I haven't let you down. I hope I haven't—"

"Not a chance." He sent her the broad smile she
remembered so well from her childhood. "We're both
extremely proud of you. We just want to see you
happy, that's all."

Jennifer stared at him, her eyes still swimming with
tears. As much as she wanted to, she couldn't reassure him, couldn't tell him she *was* happy. How could
she be when there existed a vacant place inside her, a
place that ached for something she'd lost a long time
before?

So instead, she smiled and told him she loved him.

Chapter Seven

"Boy, are you on edge."

Jennifer glared over her shoulder at her business partner. "I'm not. I'm just..." An adequate excuse for her behavior of the past four and a half hours didn't spring to mind, and she scowled. "Butt out, Susan."

"Right, you're not on edge, not at all." Susan laughed. "It's because you're seeing *him* this afternoon, isn't it?"

Jennifer lifted her eyebrows in an attempt at the haughtiness Susan had turned into an art form. "Him? I'm sure I don't know who you mean."

Susan laughed again. "Your old boyfriend, that's who."

Jennifer gritted her teeth. *So much for haughty.* "He's not...he wasn't..." She gave up. "What I said before, Susan, the thing that had to do with a part of your anatomy, it goes double now. I'll be in my office.''

Cheeks burning, Jennifer closed her office door behind her, then leaned against it. She was in deep trouble. Ryder would be here in less than an hour, and she still hadn't figured out what had happened between them—to her—at their meeting two days ago.

She pushed away from the door and crossed to her desk. She had been obsessed with him from the moment she learned he'd returned to Hazelhurst. And the other day, she'd gone to the plant because she'd *had* to see him.

Jennifer stroked the waxy leaves of the ivy plant that spilled over the corner of her desk. She'd told herself curiosity had driven her there. Had told herself that she'd wanted to learn what had happened to him in the past ten years, things like how his hands—and his heart—had become so hard.

Curiosity seemed a sensible reason. A safe, expected response considering their shared past.

Jennifer frowned. Expected? Sensible and safe? Lord, nothing in the past week had been expected, and as for sensible and safe... well, even letting those two words filter through her brain in association with Ryder was nothing short of ludicrous.

The terrible truth was, it was still between them. The chemistry. The electricity. She didn't want it to be true, but she knew enough to admit some forces of nature couldn't be stopped.

But they could be controlled.

Jennifer straightened her shoulders. All she needed to do was remember the past, remember the way he'd lied, what he'd done to Sonny, then remind herself why he was back in Hazelhurst.

A trembling sensation settled in the pit of her stomach. No problem.

And as for the other day, she rationalized, he'd taken her by surprise. That's all. He hadn't played fair, giving her no warning before his mouth touched hers. If he had, she wouldn't have behaved so...wantonly.

Sure. Jennifer's cheeks burned as she remembered the way she'd parted her lips in invitation, the way she'd gripped his shoulders for support as she sagged against him.

Jennifer whirled away from the desk, furious. Blasted man! If he'd been a gentleman, she could have neatly avoided the whole thing.

But when had Ryder Hayes ever been a gentleman?

Her heart sank at the truth of that even as she heard the jangle of the bell above the office door. She checked her watch; it was still early for Ryder. Maybe the postman had forgotten to deliver something, she thought hopefully. Or maybe it was another client, or—

Her intercom buzzed and her heart sank again. *So much for maybes.* Sucking in a deep, steadying breath, Jennifer grabbed her briefcase and headed out to meet Ryder.

Outside in the reception area, Ryder took in his own deep breath and slipped his hands into his pockets, bracing himself for that first stunning moment when he would see her.

He told himself his behavior more than bordered on adolescent. He assured himself that, this time, Jennifer Joyce would have no effect on him.

Her door swung open, she stepped into the room, and a freight train hit him in the gut. The sensation was one of speed and heat and déjà vu. It took his breath, it took his sanity. Ryder curled his fingers into his palms and prayed it didn't show.

She wore linen again, this time in a vibrant tangerine color. The skirt flared softly, giving him only a glimpse of her delectable knees. The jacket was short, stylish and showed off her small waist. Contrasting to the rough texture of the suit, her creamy-colored blouse looked as if it would be silky under his fingers—he shifted his gaze to the soft patch of flesh exposed by the blouse's open neck—like her skin would be.

"Ryder." Jennifer stopped in front of him, finding herself oddly breathless. "I didn't expect you for another thirty minutes."

What could he tell her? That he'd been so anxious for this moment that he'd raced through his meetings and skipped lunch? He could hardly admit it to himself. He cleared his throat. "I became available earlier than I'd expected, so I thought I would just...come now. But...if this isn't convenient for you—"

"No," Jennifer murmured, aware that both Susan and Patti were hanging on every word and that they knew she had nothing else on her schedule. "Now is fine. If you're ready?"

He was and they stepped out into the warm spring day.

When the door had clicked shut behind them, Ryder turned toward her, clearing his throat once more. "I haven't had lunch yet, would you mind stopping somewhere to get a burger or something?"

Her pause lasted only a heartbeat, but it was long enough for Ryder to interpret. Anger burned through him. "We could go somewhere no one would see you with me," he said stiffly. "I don't even object to a drive-through, if it would make you feel better."

Heat stung her cheeks at both his assumption and the grain of truth in it. "Don't be ridiculous," she said, too sharply for the normalcy she wanted to project. "We'll go to the Short Stack Café."

Located several doors down from her office, the Short Stack was a traditional downtown diner and had been a Hazelhurst institution since it had opened in the mid-fifties.

And everyone in town stopped at the diner, if only occasionally. The town gossips stopped a lot more often than that. Ryder arched an eyebrow. "Small towns talk, Jen."

"We're doing business, Ryder." She pushed her hair away from her face. The breeze tossed it back. "There's no reason we shouldn't be seen together."

He shrugged. "Fine by me. Of course, I never did care about appearances."

His inference that she did rankled. She tamped the emotion back and let out her breath in a short huff. "You remember where the café is?"

"How could I forget?" He grinned at her and started up the street toward the diner. "Remember, I worked there for a while."

Jennifer found herself grinning back. "A week, to be exact."

"So, I wasn't the world's greatest busboy."

"Or dishwasher. Or waiter."

"Right." Ryder looked around him as they walked. "I see time's stood still in Hazelhurst."

Jennifer glanced around her, trying to see the downtown area through Ryder's eyes. In a strange way he was right, nothing had changed. Sinclaire's dress shop was still on the corner, that Pepto-Bismal-pink sign still hung above the entrance to Marlena's Palace of Hair Care and Beauty and the gazebo on The Green was still in need of a coat of paint.

Jennifer drew her eyebrows together in thought. Whether Ryder realized it or not, more than those obvious things were unchanged in Hazelhurst. Thursday evenings in the summer there were still free concerts on The Green, the same gossip was shared at the beauty shop and corner drugstore as had been shared ten years ago, kids still cruised Buckeye Street on boring Saturday nights.

And The Creek was still the wrong side of the tracks.

Time had indeed stood still.

"Here we are," Ryder murmured.

Jennifer realized she'd been about to walk right past the café and blinked in surprise. "Yes," she said unnecessarily, and stepped through the door he held open for her.

The café's interior was a mishmash of original fifties' colors and patterns and every other style that had been popular when something had worn out and needed to be replaced. But the food had remained the same—an all-American meal that filled the stomach without emptying the wallet.

Conversation in the nearly full diner ceased as they stepped inside. Ryder shot a glance at Jennifer. Obviously he'd been recognized. Also obvious was the fact that the citizens of Hazelhurst would be whispering and speculating for days to come about what was going on between Henry Joyce's daughter and that no-good Hayes kid.

The same as they'd speculated way back when.

The first available booth was located at the rear of the restaurant and they started toward it. "Hi, Mrs. Willis," Jennifer called, ignoring the fish-eye the woman sent her. "How's Sally Ann? And Betsy? I haven't gotten their reunion reservations back, I hope they're planning to attend?"

The woman murmured that they were, and Jennifer moved on, nodding to this one, pausing to speak with that one. Some of the people's names he recognized although he couldn't place any of the faces.

But where he'd heard a name before wasn't what interested him. Jennifer was. For even as she exchanged pleasantries and familiarities, he noticed that the warmth in her voice didn't entirely reach her eyes.

It was as if she held herself slightly away from others, even when those others were people she called friends.

They slipped into the booth and Ryder narrowed his own eyes as he considered her. She wasn't being insincere, not deliberately anyway. Nor, he knew, was she playing a game. It was almost as if—

"Why are you looking at me like that?" she whispered, plucking the menus from their resting place between the condiments and handing him one.

"Truth?" He looked at her over the top of the laminated card. She nodded and he answered, "I was analyzing you."

She frowned. "Analyzing me? Why?"

"I think that should be obvious—there was something between us once, ten years have passed."

"We were friends."

"Oh, right. I forgot."

He returned his gaze to the menu, and she stared at the top of his head a moment before making a sound of annoyance. "And did your analysis unearth something deep and dark that I should know about?"

The waitress came then and took their order. Jennifer exchanged a few words with her, ignoring the woman's obvious desire for an introduction. When she'd left, Jennifer looked back at Ryder. "Well?"

Ryder tapped the menu against the scarred tabletop. "I don't think you really want to know my opinion."

"Shouldn't I be the judge of that?"

He tossed the menu aside. "All right, then. You don't care anymore. Or don't want to."

Jennifer stared at him, nonplussed. "Pardon me?"

He shrugged. "You were always a friendly person, but it was more than being outgoing. You liked people, you really cared about them—how they felt, what was happening in their lives. Now it feels superficial, it feels just . . . friendly."

Jennifer stared at him, a trembling sensation in the pit of her stomach. Fury, she told herself. She was furious with him—for his arrogance, his cold-blooded overconfidence.

She carefully set her own menu aside, using the moments to collect herself, then met his gaze. "I don't appreciate you coming back to town—"

"Obviously."

"And analyzing me after two short meetings."

"Today makes three. Besides, you wanted to know."

"My point is the same. I—" She bit off the words as the waitress returned with their soft drinks, continuing when she left again. "You have no idea who I am. No idea—"

"But I thought I knew who you were," he inserted quietly. "Up until the end, anyway."

The end. Sonny's death. Jennifer opened her briefcase and pulled out the list of properties she'd arranged to show him today. She wouldn't allow him to tie her into knots. She wouldn't allow him to affect her. She had allowed both once and all it had brought her was pain.

"As you probably already know," she said stiffly, "the economy here hasn't been so great in the last couple of years. Because of that I have some stellar properties at well below previous market values. Several of the ones I'm going to show you today are available as lease purchases and are great buys. This one—'' she held out a flyer ''—has an adorable paneled study. The kitchen is renovated and completely built—''

"Cut the cheerful little selling act, Jen. You don't have to convince me of anything."

She flushed and snatched the flyer back. "But I think I do. It's my job, remember?"

"Sure, but that's not what the last two minutes were all about. You're using this—'' he gestured to the flyer she'd just showed him ''—as a way to keep our conversation impersonal. What exactly are you trying to avoid?"

She glared at him, furious that he could read her so easily, furious that he was right. "The only reason we're sitting here is because you have acquired my services as a Realtor."

"Talk a little louder, Jen, I don't think the people up front heard you."

"I don't care what the people of this town think."

"That's bull, you always cared. It's why you were one of Sonny's girls and not mine."

He hadn't meant to say that, but now that the words, the thought, was between them, he would deal with it. "Got a comeback for that one?"

She didn't and she stared at him, shaken. "I don't know what you mean."

"No?" He leaned across the table and caught her hands. "What about the Keighton place?"

She tugged against his grasp. "Let me go."

"Is it there among the flyers? Did you even think about it at all?"

She tipped her chin up. "Yes, I thought about it, and I decided—"

"That it wouldn't be right," he mimicked, releasing her hands. "Sonny's memory might be sullied."

"That's not it! It's—"

"What *are* you afraid of? Resurrecting Sonny's ghost or remembering the truth?"

"Stop it!" she hissed, gripping the edge of the table. "I'm not afraid. I don't want to talk about Sonny, that's all. I don't want to talk about him, I don't want to think about him. Besides, you're a fine one to talk about the truth!"

"I always faced it, Jen. Not like you, you've only evaded it. You're evading it now."

"I'm leaving." She began gathering her things, her hands shaking almost uncontrollably.

"Running, you mean."

"Damn you, Ryder." Jennifer stood, fighting the tears that filled her eyes and threatened to overflow. "It was always like this between us. Always—"

She shook her head, unable to say any more without totally shaming herself by bursting into tears. Grabbing her briefcase, she turned and fled the restaurant.

Once outside she drew in a deep breath and, not knowing where else to go, started across the street and for The Green. She made it all the way to its center and the gazebo before Ryder caught up with her.

He climbed the three steps and crossed to where she stood, holding on to one of the ornately turned posts as if it were a lifeline and staring out at a view she no doubt knew by heart.

He stopped beside her, but she didn't turn his way. He studied her lovely profile, acknowledging the way her troubled expression twisted his gut.

"We need to talk."

"No," she said wearily. "We need to be apart. Leave me alone, Ryder."

He didn't give her what she asked, instead he too stared out at the empty green, using the moments to decide what he was going to say to her and how he was going to say it. He'd come to Hazelhurst to put a part of his life—the most unpleasant part—to rest. To do that, he couldn't leave Jennifer alone. She was too big a part of that past.

While in the diner the sky had clouded over and a wind had kicked up. The birds, which would have been sweetly singing before, were now curiously quiet, their song replaced by the rustle of the leaves and the heavy beat of his own heart.

Ryder turned back to her. "You were right, inside, about it always being like this between us. Fiery, combustible. Sometimes out of control." He took a deep breath. "And Sonny was always between us, too. He still is."

The breeze stirred her hair, and need curled through him. The need to touch her, to smooth the coppery strands then muss them again, this time with his fingers. Ryder fought the needs off. To give in would only complicate an already difficult situation.

"Why won't you talk about him, Jen? He was a big part of our lives—maybe the biggest. He *shaped* our lives back then."

When she tried to look away, he caught her chin and gently turned her face to his. "Do you ever talk about him? With Cyndi? Meredith?"

She gazed at him, her soft brown eyes brimming with tears. His breath caught at the helplessness of her expression, at what he read in their depths. Swearing, Ryder dropped his hand and turned away. "He's still Saint Sonny, isn't he? He's crystallized in your mind as the perfect hero. The golden boy who strutted onto a football field and brought us all to glory."

"Stop it!" her voice broke. "Please, Ryder, just...stop."

He swung back around, meeting her eyes. "Why should I, Jennifer? Just tell me why."

"Because—" She bit back the words, staring at him in horror. She'd never told anyone the truth, never told anyone about her last meeting with Sonny. She sank onto one of the benches and dropped her head into her hands. She drew in a deep, shuddering breath, then looked back up at him. "Because it's my fault Sonny died."

Ryder stared down at her, too shocked to speak. Seconds ticked past, and as they did, anger replaced shock. He took a step back, curling his fingers into his palms as he did. "I thought I was the one who killed Sonny. You accused me of it—the whole damn town did."

She clasped her hands in her lap. "It wasn't like that. It—"

''The hell it wasn't! I lived it, babe.'' He spun away from her and crossed to the opposite side of the gazebo. Breathing deeply, fighting for control, he stared out at the gray horizon.

When he had himself and his emotions in check, he turned back to her once more. ''I nearly died, too. But no one gave a damn about that. I came out of a coma to the news that I'd killed my best friend. That's not something a guy can forget or confuse. So don't sit there and try to tell me otherwise, not about that, Jennifer.''

Her chest ached with unshed tears, with past pain and guilt. ''You don't know the whole story, nobody does.'' She wrapped her arms around herself. ''Sonny came to me that night, at the after-prom party. He told me he loved me.'' The other things he'd told her jumped to her tongue. She swallowed them, her tears spilling silently over. ''I could tell he was confused...upset. He needed a friend, he needed me. I turned him away.''

''He told you he loved you?'' Ryder almost choked on the words.

''Yes.''

''What about Cyndi?''

When she only lowered her eyes, Ryder swore. Guilt was the invisible thread that bound her to Sonny still. Not just guilt over sending Sonny away or his dying, but guilt over her own feelings for her best friend's steady. To assuage the guilt, she carried a torch.

And where had he fit in back then? Where did he fit now, in her little drama? The eternal bad guy? The weakness she whipped herself for?

Anger stunned him. Jealousy was even harder to take. He was reminded of himself at eighteen—the way the anger, the frustration, twisted inside him was the same. And even now, he wanted the release of punching Sonny out—for being selfish and callow, for betraying him.

But he couldn't punch out a ghost, just as he couldn't carry one around on his shoulder forever.

He squatted down in front of her and caught her hands once more. "Take me to Sonny's. There are ghosts there—ghosts we both need to deal with."

She met his eyes, knowing hers were red-rimmed and wet. "Why can't you leave this alone?"

"Because I can't," he said simply. "Because neither of us can afford to."

He brought her hands to his mouth then, and she shuddered. His lips were warm, his chin scratchy. She wanted to cradle her head against his chest and have him stroke her hair and whisper soft, comforting words.

But she wasn't a child, and he wasn't for her. Even acknowledging those truths, denial was an agony.

"Do you have the key?" He saw by her expression that she did. Hands still joined, he stood, bringing her with him. "We need to do this, Jennifer. Take me there."

The drive to the Keighton's north-side home took less than ten minutes. Jennifer and Ryder didn't speak, not during the drive over, not when Jennifer stopped the car in front of the Tudor-style house.

Hands trembling, she turned off the ignition. "Here we are," she murmured.

"Yes." Ryder grasped the door handle but didn't pull it.

Jennifer cleared her throat, but even so, when she spoke her voice was a husky whisper. "I haven't been inside since the day...of...the funeral. I don't even drive by if I can avoid it." She clasped her hands in her lap. "That day, I helped Mrs. Keighton...serve sandwiches and coffee. It helped take my mind off...you know."

He did. Ryder looked up at the elegant house. He could imagine how it had been that day. He pictured fragile Cyndi, shattered; introspective Meredith, totally withdrawn. And Jennifer, a frenzy of activity.

A lump formed in his throat. "He was my friend, too. At least I..." This time it was he who shook his head and let a thought trail off. "Everyone forgot that. They were so busy making me into the villain—" He met her eyes. "I never got to say goodbye."

Warmth bloomed inside her. Warmth and understanding and tenderness. She tried to hold them back, they filled her despite the effort. Chest aching, she laid a hand on his arm. "What happened the night of the prom? You and Sonny were so angry...so ugly toward one another. All these years I've wondered..." She slid her hand down his arm until it lay over his. "What happened between you two?"

Ryder lowered his eyes to where her small hand cradled his larger one, then lifted his gaze back to meet hers, a catch in his throat. "You really don't know?"

"No."

He turned back to the house. "Let's go in."

"Then you'll tell me?"

"Maybe." He opened his door. "Someday, maybe."

They went up the walk, the once-perfect landscaping now irregular and slightly overgrown. Mrs. Keighton had been obsessive about appearances, and she'd always placed a decoration on the polished mahogany front door—a different one for every holiday and season. Today's would have been a brilliant spring wreath, Jennifer thought, gazing at the naked wood. It would have been lovely but a little too grand to really welcome.

Jennifer fumbled for a moment with the keys and the lock, then the door swung open. They stepped inside.

The ghosts were there, in the large empty foyer and in every other room of the house. They wandered through each, not speaking, and Jennifer knew Ryder was as engrossed in the ghosts, the memories, as she.

And as she looked around, her chest tightening, remembrances swept over her—of jokes shared, of the expression on one of their faces when none of the adults were looking, of Sonny's smiles and Ryder's smoldering gaze.

Suddenly it all came crashing in on her, smothering her—the stale air, the memories, the awareness of Ryder by her side.

"I've got to get out of here," Jennifer whispered, swinging around and running from the room. She raced down the circular staircase, through the front parlor and tugged open the door to the patio. Outside at last, she gulped in the fresh air.

Ryder followed her. He came up behind her, stopping close enough to touch but not touching. For long minutes they gazed out at the large, wooded backyard.

"Did you cry?" she asked finally, softly.

"Yes," he admitted softly. "Did you?"

"All summer." She tipped her head back to meet his eyes. "I grew up that summer."

"I grew old."

Not knowing what to say, if indeed there was anything to say, she turned back to the view.

The silence stretched between them, this time Ryder broke it. "Do you remember that last Halloween party?"

"Mmm."

"I came as James Dean."

Jennifer smiled a little at the memory. "You *were* James Dean."

"You and Cyndi and Meredith came as Charlie's Angels."

The laugh that bubbled to her lips surprised her. "Don't remind me."

"We were kids."

"We were so young."

Ryder gave in to the need then and laid his hands on her shoulders. She stiffened and for a split second he thought she would move away. Then she relaxed and leaned back against his chest. Nothing in the past ten years had felt quite so right.

"Mrs. Keighton always went all out with the decorations." Jennifer smiled wistfully. "I loved the luminaries and jack-o'-lanterns best. Remember how she lined the walks and drives with them?"

"Yes." He brushed his thumbs ever so softly against the nape of her neck. "How about the scavenger hunt Sonny trumped up?"

Jennifer bit back a sigh as Ryder began to move his fingers in slow, soft sweeps. "An excuse for couples to sneak off and neck."

As the words passed her lips, she regretted them. They brought to mind a memory that she knew he, like she, couldn't forget.

She heard his softly drawn breath, and against her shoulder she felt the wild pounding of his heart. Her words, the memory of that night, crackled in the air between them. Just when she thought he would let it die, he spoke.

"That was the first time I touched you."

Jennifer shuddered, every detail of that moment racing over her, filling her head. There had been the dark and the excitement, the snap of the cold air against her cheeks and the warmth of Ryder's hands as they'd caressed her.

And of course, there had been her response—wild and terrifying and miraculous.

"Ryder—" She tried to pull away, but he drew her back against him.

"I thought I was going to die," he murmured, his voice thick, "right there on the spot." He slipped his hands under her jacket and lowered them until they barely skimmed over her breasts. Through her silky blouse, he felt her nipples tighten. Arousal kicked him in the gut. "I touched you just like this . . . do you remember?"

Jennifer made a sound, he wasn't sure whether of pleasure or denial or both, then dropped her head back against his shoulder.

"Touching you was better than anything in the world. After that night—" Ryder skimmed his hands over her again, torturing the twin peaks, torturing himself in the process "—I couldn't stop thinking of this . . . of stroking your breasts—"

He pressed his lips to the side of her throat, drinking in her taste and texture, her scent "—of cupping them, of tasting them—"

He found the pulse that beat wildly behind her ear and tasted it with his lips and tongue "—And your legs . . . God, Jen, I couldn't sleep for wanting to caress them . . . to have them wrap around me."

He settled his hands fully over her breasts and Jennifer whimpered. She should end this, she should break away from his touch.

But all the shoulds that ran through her head were nothing compared to the fire that licked at her veins. Her pulse throbbed, her body burned. She ached in a way she only had when in this man's arms.

Jennifer lifted her hands and covered his with her own, letting him know without words how much his touch excited her and that she didn't want him to stop.

This time it was Ryder who made a sound of pleasure. He turned her to face him. "I've never forgotten touching you. Not one nuance. I remember every time—every stroke of my flesh against yours, the taste of your mouth against mine, the fragrance of your hair, the—''

With a groan he took her mouth.

At the touch of his lips Jennifer pulled a fraction away, gazing up at him in shock for a moment before drawing his mouth back to hers. How could one man's kiss be different from all others? she wondered dizzily, lifting her hands to his hair, curling her fingers in its soft thickness. How could its effect be so much more shattering? And how had she forgotten this heat? This bliss?

Jennifer pressed herself against him, against his arousal, a wellspring of memories pouring over her. Not unpleasant memories this time, not oppressive. But just as real and maybe more poignant. There were colors and scents and sensations—the joy of being young, the fear of wanting so badly she would toss aside all inhibitions, the sweet pain of that first, heady arousal.

In that moment she realized that no other man's kiss had ever affected her, that no other man had ever touched her. She had pretended there wasn't a hollow place inside, a door unopened.

But now that the door had been reopened, what was she to do?

''Jen...Jen...'' Ryder trailed kisses over her cheekbones and eyebrows, along the side of her neck, behind her ear. ''It's been so long...''

The past. Ten long years.

Jennifer flattened her hands against his chest. This was wrong. Then, because of Sonny. Now, because she knew better. ''No, Ryder.'' She drew away from him, struggling to even her breathing. "Ten years is too much to span. It wasn't right then, and it isn't now."

Ryder fought to calm his own runaway heartbeat. He searched her expression. Her desire was undeniable, as was her determination. He'd never wanted a woman the way he wanted her, had never been as moved by the touch of a hand or mouth.

But she was right—this was wrong. Crazy. He'd come back to Hazelhurst to drum her once and for all out of his life, his head. Not to once again entangle himself in something that had the power to destroy him.

Need tightened in his groin as her eyes, heavy lidded with desire, lowered to his mouth. *To hell with self-preservation.* He hauled her back against his chest and found her lips once more. Her head fell back, she parted her lips.

But in her response he felt resistance, as well as acceptance. In a way—as it always had been—it was up to him. He could convince her, he could coax and woo her.

But that wasn't good enough. It hadn't been ten years ago when he'd still been a boy, it certainly wasn't now that he was a man.

He set her away from him. "This was a mistake."

"Yes." She buried her fingers into the cotton of his pullover.

He drew in a far from steady breath. "It won't happen again."

"No." She flattened her fingers against his chest, then dropped her hands, acknowledging that she felt as if she were being torn in two. "Never again."

He wanted to tell her that never was a long time, but he saw by the expression in her eyes that he didn't have to. He tipped his face to the sky. "The rain will be here soon."

Jennifer followed his glance. In a way it had been raining for a long time, she thought. The past moments had been ones of sunshine. She shook her head. Remembered sunshine. Not the real thing, not a new day.

Jennifer pulled a shaking hand through her hair. "Should we...what would you like to do now?"

What he would like was out of the question. Ryder sighed. "Let's look at the other properties."

She wanted to refuse. Wanted to run, to hide, to forget the past minutes had ever happened. Trying to turn back the clock was wasted effort; she should know. "Fine," she agreed. "We better go, then."

Within minutes they had locked the door to Sonny's house and started down the walk.

Chapter Eight

The figures didn't look good, none of them. Ryder frowned and pushed away from his desk. Dammit, he had hoped for better. Much better.

Tossing down his pencil, he stood and stretched, his body aching from too many hours without a break. He'd stayed long after everyone else had left, wanting to go over the numbers again, sure there was something he'd missed.

There wasn't.

He pressed the heels of his hands to his eyes. The cost of raw materials had risen dramatically over the past few years, and he projected that trend to continue. With no nearby port, shipping into and out of Hazelhurst wasn't easy or cheap. The shop itself was in good working order, although in a few years, equipment would have to start being replaced, and heating the plant during the winter months was a controller's nightmare.

Ryder frowned. Compound those problems with the fact that the union had the corporation in a bear hug, with rumors of a wage-increase demand come next contract, and he had what appeared to be a no-win situation on his hands.

No-win for Hazelhurst, that was. The corporation always won. They paid people like him well to make sure of it.

He crossed to the window. This plant was it. The main job supplier for Hazelhurst. Close the plant, Hazelhurst withered then died. Ryder dragged his hands through his hair. The Short Stack, after thirty-odd years of business, would probably close. Sinclaire's dress shop, the corner drugstore, Marlena's beauty parlor. One giant snowball gaining in size and speed, all because of a decision it was his job, his responsibility, to make.

He swore and swung away from the window. Another American town bowing to the skill and efficiency of the Japanese. More good people on welfare, some on the street.

Frustrated, Ryder thought of the guys in the shop— good guys, all of them, family men. He thought of McPherson's new baby, of Tony Morelli's pride in his new—and first—mortgage.

All shot to hell.

Jennifer.

He curled his hands into fists. She would never understand, never believe he'd done all he could. No one would, not that any of them mattered.

He'd always be the villain.

Swearing, he grabbed his jacket. He slammed out of his office, flipping off lights as he did. The shop was quiet, the plant having long ago stopped working anything but first shift. Joyce should have realized then....

Ryder shook off the thought. No one man could be blamed for this situation—really, no man at all. The times, the attitude of manufacturing beginning way back with the dawn of the Industrial Age, modern-day unions—they all added up to make a recipe for an American disaster.

Ryder flexed his fingers. He wanted to punch someone or something, wanted to shout—

He wanted to be part of the solution instead of the problem.

Jerking on the leather jacket, Ryder stepped out into the cool night air. Tonight he would have to content himself with riding against the wind, riding until his body ached and his face burned, until absolute exhaustion made sleep less of an impossibility.

He ended up at Jennifer's house instead.

Engine still purring beneath him, Ryder stared up at her bungalow. Lights burned from half a dozen windows. She was home, she was up.

This was nuts. Insane. He had promised himself after their last meeting that he would stay as far away from her as possible, but here he was, sitting in front of her house at an hour well past respectable for calling.

But he'd promised himself the same before, on a night that reminded him of this one for no reason other than that he'd come for Jennifer.

He sucked in a sharp breath, pushing that memory aside, settling on another one. Nearly thirty days had passed since she'd taken him to Sonny's, nearly a month had passed since he'd held her, kissed her... it had been agony.

Ryder frowned. How had he gone ten years without holding her? That fact seemed inconceivable to him now, and even more so was the notion of spending the next ten years counting the seconds and minutes that had passed without her.

He shook his head. After they'd left Sonny's, the rest of the afternoon had passed with them exchanging barely a word. They had parted coolly, with his assurance that he would call when he'd come to a decision. He hadn't called and neither had she.

In truth, he hadn't thought about the properties at all—he'd been too busy thinking about her. She'd knocked him for a loop. Touching her had transported him back ten years. He'd been eighteen again and wildly in love with one of the most popular girls in school.

Repeatedly over the past weeks, he'd told himself that his feelings were normal, that they were to be expected. Unfinished emotional business, that's all it was. He and Jennifer had parted with every nerve ending exposed and raw. It was logical that, at first, he would react to her like dynamite did to a lit match.

But all his assurances hadn't helped him regain his footing, hadn't relieved the ache. And like a fool, he'd driven by Sonny's house every day. Irrationally hoping to see her, masochistically reliving the moment between them on the patio. And each time, the need to make love with her became more pronounced, more debilitating.

Ryder slipped off his helmet and tunneled his fingers through his hair, looking up at the house again. What was between them was undeniably explosive, and like anything that had that much power, it was dangerous. Only a fool toyed with dynamite.

Tonight he was a fool.

It wasn't the first time.

Ryder frowned again, thinking of the night he'd refused to think about moments before, the night of the prom. He remembered how his heart had beat drumlike in his chest as he'd pulled his bike to a stop in front of the gymnasium, remembered how his hands had shaken as he'd cut the engine.

This was it, he'd thought, staring up at the gym's row of double doors. Jennifer was in there. He was going to find her and tell her once and for all how he felt. Then he would ask her if he had a chance. If he didn't, he would say goodbye. To her. To Hazelhurst. There was nothing left here for him.

As he swung off the bike, Sonny pushed through the gym's doors and zigzagged down the steps. "Ryder, my man," he called. "Just the dude I wanted to see."

Ryder folded his fingers into his palms, anger shooting through him. Twenty-four hours ago, he would have been happy to see the other boy, but twenty-four hours ago he had called him friend.

Sonny, still in his tux, stopped next to the bike and grinned. "What do you say, buddy. Let's blow this grammar school gig and do some real partying."

"What's with the buddy crap?" Ryder returned, his voice tight. "I thought my credit had run out."

"A misunderstanding." Sonny smiled and dragged his hands through his blond hair. "It happens. Right man?"

Ryder narrowed his eyes. Sonny seemed different tonight, slightly off center or skewed. "Where's Cyndi?"

"Cyndi's a drag. Come on, ace. Let's ride."

"Sorry, Sonny-boy, but I've got a date. I don't desert *my* dates."

As Ryder made a move to step around him, Sonny plucked the bike keys from his fingers. He jiggled them tauntingly. "I thought we'd been through that. Give it up. Jennifer's not for you."

Ryder curled his fingers into his palms, adrenaline pumping into him until he shook with it. "I'm going to fight for her," he said softly, dangerously. "So you'd better get out of my way...now."

Sonny laughed, the sound almost wild against the night air. "Fight for her? Why bother? What would she want with a punk like you, a loser?"

Ryder drew his fist back, but even as he pictured it smashing into Sonny's face, even as he felt the sweet satisfaction contact would bring, he dropped it and took a step away from the other boy. He had come for Jennifer, not to settle a score with Sonny.

So he faced his old friend. "You're scared, aren't you? You've never had to fight for anything, it's all been given to you. You don't even know how. And now you're about to face the real world and you have no idea what to do.''

''You've got it all wrong.'' Sonny laughed again, but this time the nervous edge was unmistakable. ''I'm going to have it all, man. I'm going to be a success.''

''Oh, yeah? Then why do you look like you're going to throw up? Face it, man. It's over. Maybe you can fool three teenage girls with your smile and free-flowing bull, but girls grow up...their eyes open up.'' Ryder held out his hand. ''Give me the keys.''

''You're so sure she'll choose you?'' Sonny demanded. ''A guy who's going to end up working in the factory, just like his old man.''

''Give me the keys, Sonny.'' Ryder made a grab for them. Sonny jerked his hand back, laughing again.

''Fearless, Ryder,'' he taunted, weaving on his feet. ''You don't have to follow the rules, do you? You can do whatever you please, no one to answer to, no responsibilities. People expect things of me, man. I've always got to be perfect, always got to do the right thing. Well, you know what I think?'' He swung onto the bike. ''I think you're full of it. You're a fake. You care what everybody thinks, you care big time. You want to be me.''

Ryder felt Sonny's words like a blow to his solar plexus. He took a step backward as he realized Sonny was right. ''I don't know what you pumped into your system toni—''

''Reality, man. A little dose of the grown-up world.'' Sonny fitted the keys into the ignition. ''Prove you're not a fake. Prove you don't care what any of these bastards think. Let's ride." When Ryder paused, Sonny twisted the throttle, revving the engine. "What's the matter? Afraid your *girlfriend* won't be around when you come back? If she's not, what'll that tell you, buddy?"

Ryder had gotten onto the bike. And even as he'd done so he had known it was madness, had known that Sonny had manipulated him again.

But he hadn't known how right he'd been about Sonny's mood, his fears. That knowledge had come with hindsight.

Ryder jiggled the keys in his hands and looked back up at Jennifer's house. He'd never gotten the chance to tell her how he felt. Like everything else that had happened that night, it had eaten at him for ten years. And if he let it eat away long enough, one day there would be nothing left.

It was time.

Ryder swung off the bike and started up her walk.

Jennifer answered the door on the second knock. Minutes ago she'd heard the bike and had peeked out the window to see him staring up at her house. She'd dealt with her emotions then—the giddy rush of joy, as well as the apprehension, the panic and the pleasure.

But, strangely, surprise hadn't been one of those emotions. He'd been on her mind all evening, even more than the way he'd dominated her thoughts for weeks now. And something about the cool snap of the air had reminded her of that spring night so long ago when he had come to her window.

He smiled at her now, the curving of his lips easy, unabashedly masculine. She gripped the edge of the door with her right hand. How, she wondered, could such a casual gesture promise such a wealth of complications? And how could something so simple affect her so strongly?

She lowered her eyes, more out of self-preservation than curiosity. His stance was as easy as his smile and so reminiscent of the cocky young man from her past—hands slipped into the front pockets of faded jeans, legs spread, head tilted slightly to the side.

But just as they had all those years ago, his eyes gave him away. She clutched the door a little tighter. "What's wrong?"

"Hello, Jen."

She drew her eyebrows together and searched his expression. "Ryder?"

"Can I come in?"

Without hesitation, Jennifer stepped away from the door.

Ryder followed her inside. He trailed his gaze over her, lingering, she thought, on her mouth and the wide neck of her oversize T-shirt. Her pulse scrambled, and she reached up to smooth her hair.

He shrugged out of his jacket. "Nice place. It looks like you."

"Thanks." She folded her arms across her chest. "How did you find me?"

"The phone book."

"Of course." Feeling silly, she motioned to her right. "Come on in."

She led him into the living room. "Can I get you anything? A glass of wine or a beer? Coffee?"

"Beer would be good." He met her eyes then, and her pulse raced at the look in his. She turned and hurried from the room.

When she returned with their drinks, he was standing in front of her fireplace, staring at the framed pictures that lined the mantel. She paused in the doorway, watching as he picked up this photo and that, studying one then another.

She moved her gaze over him, from the place where his dark hair brushed the back of his neck, across his broad shoulders and down to where his jeans hugged his trim hips.

Her pulse points tickled, as did another point—one lower, more intimate. Jennifer shifted uncomfortably. Letting him in had been madness. Not that she worried he would try to harm her, but because he made her vulnerable. He made her feel young and willing to take chances. He made her forget the past.

As if he sensed her presence, Ryder turned and met her gaze. She could tell by the expression in his that he knew she'd been there for several moments, watching him. Heat stung her cheeks. "Here we go," she said, crossing the room, forcing brightness.

She handed him the beer, and their fingers brushed. He turned back to the photos. He touched one of the frames with the same fingers that had just touched hers, and her abdomen tightened.

"Pretty kids. Whose are they?"

Jennifer jerked her gaze back to his, her cheeks coloring. "My brother's." She cleared her throat. "They're only thirteen months apart, and hellions."

"Christopher has kids?" Ryder turned back to the image. "It's hard to believe."

"I know." She went to the edge of the couch and perched, holding her glass of wine in a death grip. "He got married his freshman year of college. He's an engineer for a car manufacturer in Detroit. I don't get to see them as often as I'd like."

Ryder took a long swallow of the beer. Silence stretched between them—taut and uncomfortable and electric. He hadn't even touched her, yet every part of her body throbbed for something only he could give her.

She followed his lead, taking a sip of her wine. It seemed icy against her parched throat. She sipped again and again, stopping only when she realized he was staring at her, a question in his eyes. A question and heat. It was the heat that had her searching for something to say. "How's your family?"

Ryder leaned so his shoulders rested against the mantel. "You know my dad died?" When she nodded, he went on. "Mom's doing okay. She's working in a home for battered women." His lips twisted. "Helping other women through their hell has helped her through her own."

Jennifer swallowed past the lump in her throat. "How about your brothers and sisters?"

Ryder tapped the beer bottle lightly against the mantel. "Jon's doing well. He's a policeman in Cleveland. Meg's married with a couple of kids." Ryder rolled his shoulders. "The twins didn't fare as well—Tim's been in and out of drug rehabs for the last couple of years and Tina, well, she goes from one abusive relationship to another."

Jennifer tightened her fingers on her glass, acknowledging the ache. "I'm sorry."

He shrugged again and turned back to the rows of smiling faces on the mantel. "It's not surprising, considering what we all went through. It could be worse."

Jennifer set her wine aside and clasped her fingers together, uncertain what to say next. She would like to tell him she wasn't surprised—that he was the success story, that he'd made so much out of himself. He'd always been special—special enough not to let the worst kind of childhood get him down.

But she didn't dare say any of those, so instead she asked, "How did you get here? To this place?"

"I told you, the phone book."

"That's not what I meant."

He held her gaze a moment, then turned away. Again silence engulfed them. Jennifer watched as he moved restlessly around the room. He stopped suddenly and turned toward her.

"What about you?"

"Me?"

"Yeah. No one else stayed in Hazelhurst. Why did you?"

"Other kids from our class stayed. Bob Thompkins and Sue Meyers and—"

"That's not what *I* meant."

Meredith. Cyndi. This time it was Jennifer who lowered her eyes. She'd understood his question immediately—he meant their group.

She tipped her chin up, hating the defensive gesture but unable to check it. "My staying isn't so unusual. My family's here. And unlike you, I always enjoyed living in Hazelhurst. I care about the people here."

Ryder laughed, the sound hard and somehow lonely. "You'd be surprised, Jennifer. Hell, I even surprised myself."

He crossed back to the mantel, to a picture out of both their pasts, of two girls in cheerleading uniforms. "What about Cyndi and Meredith? How are they doing?"

"Good," Jennifer said lightly. "Cyndi's a big success—a television personality. She has her own cable show."

"Really?" Ryder picked up the photo. "What about Meredith? Is she a professor at some prestigious university or something?"

Jennifer stood then sat back down. "No... I'm really not sure... I heard she was back in college."

He turned. "You heard?"

"Mmm." She stood again, then went and collected his empty bottle from the mantel. "Another beer?"

He caught her arm, forcing her to meet his eyes. He studied her expression. His eyes, she knew, saw too much. "The three of you didn't stay friends?"

"No." Jennifer shifted her gaze. "What about that beer?"

"One's my limit."

"Well, I think I'll get myself—"

"Your glass is still full." Ryder tightened his fingers on her arm. "What happened, Jen?"

She lifted her shoulders, feigning nonchalance. "We don't talk. We . . . haven't since—"

To her own horror, her eyes filled with tears. Blinking, she tugged her arm from his grasp. She went to the window, struggling to get control of herself.

Seconds ticked past. Finally, softly, she said, "We haven't spoken, not really, since Sonny died."

"Since that summer?"

"No. Since that night." Jennifer drew in a shuddering breath. "Cyndi didn't return my calls and when we passed each other at graduation we said a few words, something like 'Hi' or 'How are you?' She went to her grandmother's for the summer, then, I guess, off to college after. Meredith disappeared. She didn't even show up for the commencement.

"It seems you were right," she finished, hearing the trace of bitterness, hating it. "We weren't really friends at all. It seems I, poor fool, was the only one who *didn't* realize it."

Ryder moved up behind her. He ran his fingers through her hair, stroking her scalp, the back of her neck. She bit back a groan, a sound of both pleasure and pain.

"I didn't say those things to hurt you, Jen. I said them because they were true, and because—"

She didn't let him finish. She whirled around, furious with him for his lies, with herself for the way she was willing to forget them when he touched her. "Really? Truth is so important to you?"

She angled her chin up. "Well, you never answered *my* question. How did you end up a controller for Lansing? You checked out of the hospital and disappeared. As far as I know, you never graduated."

"Ever heard of night school?"

"Don't be glib with me! Give me the truth, Ryder. You know, the thing you pretend to be so righteous about."

"This is a first." He laughed without humor, taking several steps back from her. "No one in this town ever wanted to hear the truth, not from me. Including you."

What was left of her control snapped, and anger blindsided her. Shaking with its force, she faced him. "Stop with the used-and-abused act. Stop dragging up the past as a way to avoid the here and now. You came to me tonight, Ryder. Not the other way around."

Her words sliced at him. She was right. That's the way it had always been—he'd gone to her again and again. Anger, shame, frustration, they all tightened inside him. He closed the distance between them once again.

"You want to hear the truth? Really, Jennifer? You want to hear about a broken boy who checked out of the hospital with nothing more than pride and pain medication that would wear off in a couple of hours? You want to hear how I had to crawl off the bus in Cleveland because I hurt so bad I couldn't stand? Or do you want me to describe the hellholes I lived in until I was well enough to find work, or about the days I didn't eat?"

A sob tore from her throat and she tried to turn away. He caught her shoulders with a grasp that would leave marks. "No, Jen, you wanted to hear it. When you're eighteen and hungry you'll do just about anything to fill your belly. Like going through trash cans or accepting smirking charity from the same kind of people you vowed to prove wrong."

"I didn't know..." She shook her head, tears streaming down her cheeks. "I didn't imagine—"

"Of course not," he said brutally, shaking her. "Because you didn't care. Not about me. Only about your precious Sonny."

"Stop it!" She flew at him then, pummeling her fists against his chest. "You lied to me! You lied about me! You touched me and I turned to fire, you kissed me and I forgot who I was, where I was. But that wasn't enough, was it? You had to tell Sonny we were doing it!"

She broke away from him, her breath coming in small gasps. "That night in the country club garden, I wanted to make love, I exposed myself to you and you left me. I felt so cheap...so used. And then later, when Sonny—"

"Used?" Breathless with fury, Ryder caught her to him again, this time cupping her face in his hard palms. "You were always lent to me. I only got to borrow you now and then. Isn't that right, Jen? You were one of Sonny's girls, not mine. Didn't you tell me again and again that we were only friends?"

When she tried to break away, he tightened his fingers. "You let me kiss you and fondle you when the boy you really wanted was otherwise occupied. What was it, Jen? Did you get hot for him, then let me act as a stud?''

''Damn you! It wasn't like that!'' She fisted her hands and flailed at his chest, wanting to hurt him as he hurt her. Tears scalding her cheeks, she hit at him, and when he caught her hands with his, she used her feet and knees and body to fight.

Ryder fought back, not hitting but blocking her blows. In a wrestling move, he trapped her legs with one of his and flipped her to the floor. Following her down, he pinned her under him.

With a sound wrenched from a place somewhere deep inside her, Jennifer caught her fingers in his hair and dragged his mouth to hers. She bit and clawed at him, the meeting not about love or passion but about pain and pride, about anger.

Ryder returned her fury. He thrust his tongue into her mouth, his hips against hers, the pressure of both bruising. He tasted her blood, or his own. He only dove deeper, harder.

Jennifer wrapped her legs around him and pulled at his shirt, freeing it from his jeans. She shoved at it until it was up around his shoulders, only releasing his mouth for the second it took to be rid of his pullover. But as she went to claim his lips again, he was tugging at her shirt, yanking it over her head, exposing her breasts for his hands.

Her breath caught, but she didn't pause to enjoy or savor. She fought instead with the snap of his jeans, the zipper.

And he fought with hers.

They parted but for only as long as it took to free themselves of clinging denim, then they found each other again, meeting ruthlessly, claiming, taming.

He spread her legs and thrust into her. She shouldn't have been ready but she was. She arched her back, bringing her hips to meet his—again and again.

The sounds she made, the ones he caught with his mouth and answered with ones of his own, were unfamiliar to her. They were frightening . . . primal and naked in their honesty. This was as honest as she'd ever been. With him. With anyone.

She tangled her hands in his hair, crying out with her release, with his. And in that moment, something hot and soft stole over her. Anger was replaced by heat, pain by need.

This man had always been her other half.

Exhausted, panting, she stared up at him. If she'd ever thought she could deny him, she'd been wrong. If she'd ever hoped there would come a day when she would have forgotten the cataclysm his touch conjured, she'd been a fool. Now, at this moment, she knew that whatever the future brought, a part of her would belong to him.

Ryder searched her expression, trailing his thumb lightly, gently, across her cheekbone, regret at the lone gesture of tenderness in an act that should be exquisitely so, stabbing through him. She'd deserved more, and he'd wanted to give her more.

Regret became a biting sadness—what was it with the two of them? Why couldn't they ever get it right? It was as if they were doomed to cause each other pain.

"I was yours back then," he murmured, his voice thick, touching her again, this time at the curve of her jaw. "Did you know, Jen? You were my everything...my sun and moon, my reason to go on. The night of the prom I said those things about your friends because they were true but more, because I hurt."

Ryder moved his hands to her hair, spread out on the floor around her head, and rubbed the coppery strands between his fingers. "You say Sonny loved you...but was he as faithful as I? Could he have said you were his everything? And if he had, could you have believed him?"

She thought she hadn't any more tears. She thought the fury that had consumed her minutes before would have drained her of everything. But instead she hurt more, everywhere and to the bone. This time the tears that slipped down her cheeks were from her heart instead of her gut.

"You blindly believed the other things he said. Because he was Sonny Keighton, hero, and I was just 'that boy from The Creek.'" He let the silky strands of her hair slip through his fingers. "This isn't going to work, Jen. It's not enough."

He sat up, grabbed his shirt and tugged it over his head. Jennifer followed him, crossing her arms over herself, feeling colder and more alone than she had in ten years. "Don't go, Ryder."

"I have to." He stood and pulled on his pants, slipped into his shoes. "I can't be second anymore. And I won't play number two for a ghost."

"It's not like that, Ryder." She shuddered and hugged herself tighter. "It's not."

"Isn't it?" He plucked the afghan from the back of the couch and gently wrapped it around her shoulders. "You haven't shown me otherwise. I don't think you can."

"Ryder..." She drew in a deep, shuddering breath. "Why did you come here tonight?" She made a small fluttering motion with her hand. "For this?"

He looked at her, taking in her tear-streaked face, her tangled hair and bruised mouth, and he ached, ached in a way he hadn't allowed himself to in years. "God, no. This wasn't what I wanted, wasn't how I'd dreamed..." He shook his head and shrugged into his coat. "I came here to tell you how I felt back then and because... I'm a fool."

Because I needed you. I need you still.

Jennifer read the truth in his eyes, and her breath caught. This was the way it had always been between them. When she'd opened the door tonight and seen his face, the expression in his eyes, she had known that something was wrong, that he needed her.

They'd gotten sidetracked by their past and their pain.

He was right, he was a fool. But so was she. She should let him go, but tonight they had crossed a line and there was no going back.

"You came to me," she said softly, "because we know each other. Because tonight strangers and small talk wouldn't do, because you needed a friend. That's it, isn't it?"

She saw by his expression that she was right, and although he looked away, he didn't make a move to leave.

Finally after several moments, he met her gaze once more. "For years I hated this place. You, your dad and Sonny. The hatred burned inside me. I wished the worst for this town, its inhabitants. It drove me to succeed, to overcome the odds and prove myself. Even when choosing my future, my hatred drove me. I knew the one thing everyone respected was money, and I knew the person who controlled the money was untouchable. Nobody would treat me like dirt ever again."

He laughed tightly. "I got a shock this week, Jen. You want to know what it was?"

She nodded, a trembling sensation in the pit of her stomach.

"I don't hate Hazelhurst at all."

"Oh, God." She lifted a hand to her mouth. "This is about the plant."

"It doesn't look good."

"Oh, God," she said again, hugging the afghan around her. "There's nothing to be done?"

"I don't know...it's not over yet, it's..." He let the words trail off and looked at the ceiling. "I wanted to be able to pull a rabbit out of a hat. I'd wanted—" He shook his head again and started for the door.

"What did you want, Ryder?"

He stopped but didn't turn back to her. "I used to fantasize about wreaking revenge on Hazelhurst . . . but more, I used to fantasize about saving it, about being a hero. Like your dad."

Tears welled in her eyes. Even though his back was to her, she held out a hand. ''Ryder...please. Don't go.''

''I have to.'' He looked back over his shoulder. ''Goodbye, Jen.''

As she heard the door snap shut, Jennifer dropped her head into her hands and sobbed.

Chapter Nine

Jennifer sat at her kitchen table, a cup of coffee untouched and cooling beside her. She stared at the newspaper spread out in front of her, the print blurring before her eyes. She fought the tears back, just as she'd fought them in the week that had passed since she and Ryder had made love.

No, she corrected. What they'd done had had nothing to do with love. They'd consummated an ancient passion, they'd acted on ancient history.

And once again they'd hurt each other.

She dropped her head into her hands. He hadn't contacted her. And he wouldn't, she knew. The next step would have to be hers. Only she had no idea how to make it, no idea what to do—if anything at all.

She did know one thing—she couldn't change the past. As much as she wanted and wished, it was there between them, and it always would be.

A tear escaped and slipped down her cheek. She caught it with her forefinger to the sound of the doorbell ringing. She dried her eyes and went to answer it, tamping back the absurd hope that Ryder might be standing on the other side of the door.

He wasn't.

"Mom," Jennifer said, automatically reaching up to smooth her hair. Her mother always noticed the slightest change in her appearance, and the last thing she wanted this morning was the third degree. "What are you doing here?"

Her mother smiled. "I made your favorite sticky buns this morning, and I decided to bring some by for you. I thought we might chat awhile." She cleared her throat and looked past Jennifer. "Is this a good time?"

Jennifer drew her eyebrows together. Her mother's cheeks were a bit too pink this morning, and it seemed her smile didn't quite reach her eyes. She stepped away from the door. "Sure. Come on in."

Jennifer poured them both cups of coffee and got out plates and napkins for the buns. The whole while her mother remained curiously quiet. Jennifer cast her a concerned glance. "What's on your mind, Mom?"

Mary Joyce started, her cheeks pinkening more. She shifted her gaze. "Nothing. Why do you ask?"

Jennifer crossed to the table with their coffee cups. "Because you're nervous as a cat, that's why." She set them down, then went back for their rolls. "Don't tell me crazy Mrs. Quinn's eating your flowers again?"

"I heard you're seeing that boy."

The plates slipped from her fingers, clattering to the counter. Jennifer looked back at her mother, shock rippling over her. "What did you say?"

"That you're seeing that Hayes's boy again. Pauline saw you at the Short Stack together."

Jennifer took a deep breath and counted to ten. "We're doing business, Mom. I'm helping him find a house to lease." She picked the plates back up and carried them to the table, cursing as she saw the way her hands trembled.

"Humph. Then why doesn't he call during business hours? Myra Petersen—you know, the widow who lives down the block from you—she saw him out in front of your place two nights ago. Late. She saw him go in, too. But she went to bed before he came back out."

Anger and embarrassment stung her cheeks. Jennifer worked to keep both from her voice. "She was spying on me?"

Mary Joyce leaned toward her daughter. "Hazelhurst's a small town and people talk. That's just the way it is."

"Then let them talk," Jennifer snapped, furious. "If something's going on, it's none of their business."

Her mother folded her hands primly in front of her, her expression hurt. "Is it my business? Or your father's?"

Jennifer sighed. This song and dance had a too-familiar ring. "You're my parents. I love you and care what you think. But I'm not eighteen anymore."

"I see."

Those two words spoke volumes, and Jennifer silently swore. "Mother, don't."

"Is it so wrong for your father and I to be concerned?"

"No, it's just that . . ."

Frustrated, Jennifer pushed away from the table and went back to the window over the sink. Outside, a mockingbird perched in her apple tree.

Appropriate, she thought, sighing again. Her parents would like nothing better than to have her married to some nice guy with a baby on the way. Only Ryder wasn't their idea of a nice guy. He never had been.

But he was the only guy she . . . Jennifer didn't finish the thought and looked down at her hands. She hated disappointing them, but in this one area, she had been consistent.

Jennifer drew her eyebrows together. Is that why she couldn't come out and tell her mother the truth—that even before the other night there had been something going on between her and Ryder. That there had been something going on even when she'd thought she would never see him again.

"He's stirring up trouble at the plant," her mother said quietly. "Trying to turn the men against your father. Causing problems with the union. Rumor has it the union called a secret meeting. It's been awful, honey. Just awful."

"And *where* did you hear that?" Jennifer asked, swinging back around, unable to keep the edge out of her voice.

"Your father."

"Dad?"

"Well, of course, honey. Who else?"

Jennifer stared at her mother. That wasn't right. Ryder had made it sound as if he were working to save the plant, to save her father's job. He cared about Hazelhurst, he'd convinced her of that. The way her mother talked—

"I don't know what we'll do if Henry loses that job," Mary continued, almost to herself. "He's not a young man anymore. His options are limited."

Jennifer searched her mother's expression, a knot of apprehension settling in her chest. She had never heard her parents argue, had never heard worries about finances or health or family dynamics. Everything had always been "Fine, honey." Decisions had been made and life lived with seeming effortlessness.

But now, here was her mother, obviously worried sick and reaching out, and it scared her silly.

"Dad's a successful plant manager," Jennifer said, working to sound unaffected and confident. "He has a proven track record. Even if something did happen at the plant, any company would be delighted to have him."

Mary shook her head. "He's sent out a few résumés already and hasn't even gotten a nibble in response. The other day he called a headhunter and the man said—" she took a deep breath and met her daughter's eyes "—he said your father would be difficult to place because of his age."

Jennifer's own breath caught. "But Dad's only fifty-six, that's still young, still vital. He has a lot to offer, I don't understand—"

"Younger men don't have to be paid as much. And companies don't like to hire executives who are approaching sixty-five because they won't get as many years out of them but they still have to provide retirement benefits. This headhunter also told us that some corporations even trump up reasons to let men like your father go when they near retirement age just so they don't have to pay."

"But Dad has so much experience," Jennifer rationalized. "Doesn't that count for something?" She saw by her mother's expression it didn't. It wasn't right. Her father had given thirty-plus years of service to Lansing, that should be of some value.

She swung back to the window. She'd always taken for granted that her father would work at the Hazelhurst plant until he retired. She'd always taken it for granted that everything would continue as it always had—smoothly and without a ripple.

She thought then of Ryder, of the tone of his voice when he told her what was going on at the plant, the expression in his eyes when he'd met hers.

He cared. He would make it work so no one would get hurt.

Jennifer swung back around. "Everything's going to be all right, Mom. Ryder won't let anything happen to Dad or the plant. Trust me on this."

Her mother twisted her fingers in her lap. "You really think so?"

"I do."

Mary sighed. "I never understood what you saw in that boy, but if you like him he must be a good boy...I mean, he really wouldn't try to hurt us." Mary lifted her eyes to her daughter's. "Would he?"

Jennifer stared helplessly at her mother, feeling as if she were being torn in two. "No, Mom, he wouldn't."

Her mother smiled weakly. "Thank goodness. But I wish your father could be as certain. He's not sleeping, and he's drinking too much."

"Drinking too much," Jennifer repeated. "What do you mean?"

Mary fiddled with the edge of the tablecloth. "Your father has always had a cocktail at night. You know that. But lately he has two or three and he just...stares at the television. He won't talk to me about it."

Swallowing hard, Jennifer crossed to her mother and squatted down beside her chair. "I didn't know that. Is there anything I can do?"

"No." Her mother shook her head. "Your father is so hardheaded, so proud. It's just that...his job, his position at Lansing, is so much a part of who he is. I worry that..."

"Everything's going to be fine," Jennifer reassured her awkwardly, wrapping her fingers around her mother's and squeezing. "We have to believe that. This will all blow over and later we'll wonder why we were so worried."

"How can you be so sure, Jennifer?"

Because I do know Ryder, she thought. Because I know him and I . . . love him.

Stunned, Jennifer brought a hand to her mouth. She'd fallen in love with Ryder. Despite the past and the problem with the plant, despite what she knew was best for her, she loved him.

What in the world was she going to do now?

"Jennifer, honey, what's wrong?"

She stared blankly at her mother. "I've got to go."

"But this is your house."

Jennifer glanced around her. "Then you have to go . . . I mean, there's something I have to . . . something I forgot to do."

Her mother stood and collected her purse, looking concerned. "What did you forget, honey? Is it something I can help with?"

"No, Mom. No, but thanks." Jennifer led her to the door, excitement warring with absolute, unadulterated fear. "I'll call you later, I promise." She waved, then shut the door behind her.

Turning, she rested against it. Her heart beat thundered in her chest, and she worked to catch her breath. She loved Ryder. She wanted to shout it from the rooftops. She wanted to slap herself silly for being such an idiot.

She wanted to find Ryder and kiss him senseless.

Good God, what was she going to do? Her smile faded. She couldn't tell him. Not yet. If she was sure of his feelings . . .

Jennifer shook her head. They hadn't parted under the best of terms—she almost laughed aloud at that—he'd all but said she wasn't what he needed or wanted.

But she couldn't let him, let this, just slip away. He'd loved her once, he'd told her so. He cared for her still. Maybe it could work. Maybe she could prove to him that they would be good together even after all these years.

Letting out her breath in a determined rush, she straightened her shoulders. There had to be a way, something she could do to show him how she felt. All she had to do was figure out what it was.

Ryder pushed himself harder, until the sweat poured from him and his breath came in short, deep gasps. When he could push no more, he slowed then stopped, resting his hands on his knees and breathing deeply.

Dammit, he knew better than to run during the heat of the day. But today he'd done it anyway, hoping to punish his body until he couldn't think, couldn't remember.

And more importantly, so he wouldn't feel.

He swore again. It hadn't worked. He hadn't been able to expel Jennifer from his head or his heart. No matter how hard he'd run, she'd been there. With his mind's eye he'd seen her sitting on her living room floor, the afghan wrapped around her, her eyes wide and hurt. And he heard her asking him to stay.

He loved her. He'd been an idiot to think he'd ever stopped.

Turning, Ryder started back across The Green toward the Buckeye Inn, the old downtown hotel he'd been staying at while in Hazelhurst. Maybe he should have done what she'd asked. Maybe he should have stayed and settled—

He shook his head. He'd settled for less too often in his life. He wouldn't again, even if it meant the hell of going on without her.

He pulled open the door of the aging hotel. The lobby was worn, shabby even, but still charming. Its furnishings and appointments had once been the best, so when it had aged, it had done so with grace.

He moved across the lobby toward the stairs, nodding to the desk clerk as he did. The man sent him an odd stare and he shrugged. Let him think what he liked; he wouldn't be staying much longer. If the corporation accepted his proposal, he'd be gone within the month.

Thoughts of leaving brought their own kind of pain, and Ryder shoved them resolutely away. He'd returned to Hazelhurst to come to terms with his past, not to stay, not to build a future with a part of that past. In a way he'd been successful—he understood himself and what he needed more then he ever had before, and his pride, if not his heart, was intact.

He let himself into his corner room, stopping just inside the door. Jennifer's scent—the unmistakable combination of spring flowers and fall leaves—filled his head.

He shifted his gaze to the bed. She was perched there primly and as if ready for flight, her hands folded on a brown-wrapped package in her lap. Several emotions hit him at once, not the least of which was regret that this woman would be the one woman who opened him up and made him feel everything.

She didn't smile. "Hello, Ryder."

"Jen," he said softly, tamping back the hope, holding tightly to everything but the memory of the way they'd hurt each other. "This is a surprise."

"I thought we should talk." The paper crackled as she moved her fingers. "I was afraid that after our last...meeting, you wouldn't agree to see me."

"So you broke in."

"In a way." Her cheeks colored. "The guy at the desk, Benny Wilton, we've served on a couple of committees together, and I sold him his house."

"That you're up in my room will be all over town in an hour."

She angled her chin up. "So?"

"So, you have your reputation to think of."

"To hell with my reputation."

"Big words, Jen." He shook his head slowly. "But I think you'd better go."

"I can't."

Ryder arched his eyebrows. "Can't?"

"Won't, then." She stood, set the package aside and crossed to him. She tipped her chin up and met his gaze. "You want me out, you'll have to throw me out."

Ryder stiffened, bracing himself against the need to touch her. She was so close, all he had to do was move just a fraction, and their bodies would brush; lift his hand only a smidgeon, and there she would be.

He drew a deep, steadying breath and narrowed his eyes. "What do you want from me, Jennifer?"

Everything, she thought, clasping her hands in front of her, breathless with love and uncertainty. Everything and anything. Being with you is enough.

But she couldn't say any of those things, couldn't just boldly pronounce her feelings. She swung away from him, twisting her fingers together. How should she start? Panicking, she realized she had no idea. She'd never been good at expressing her feelings, even in high school. And now, when so much rode on her words, she felt totally tongue-tied and inadequate.

She cleared her throat and met his eyes over her shoulder. "My mother stopped by this morning. She's worried about what's going on up at the plant. Apparently Dad's not handling it all too well, and she's terrified that—"

"So we're back to trying to unearth my true motives. This is great."

"No." Jennifer turned back to him and caught his arm. "That's not why I'm here. My mother wanted my assurance that everything would be all right."

"And?"

"And I gave it to her."

"Did you?" Furious, Ryder freed his arm and took a step back from her. "Then why are you here now? For assurances from me?"

"No. I—" Jennifer turned away from him, dragging her hands through her hair. How could she have bungled it so quickly?

Spit it out, she told herself. Just tell him.

Fear tightened in her chest at the thought, and she wiped her damp palms against her thighs. "I believe what you told me the other night," she whispered instead, acknowledging her own cowardice. "I believe you wouldn't purposefully hurt any of us. That's what I told my mother. I...I just wanted you to know that."

Seconds ticked past, and neither spoke or moved. Finally, softly, Ryder asked, "Is that it, Jen? Is that all you came here to tell me?"

She stared at him a moment, then turned and crossed to the bed. There, she curled her fingers around one of the ornately carved posts. "No," she replied, just as softly, simply. "I came because I can't stay away."

Still clutching the bedpost, she met his eyes. "I came today because I wanted to be with you, because staying away is torture...and because I wanted to finish what we started the other night."

Ryder didn't dare breathe. If he breathed she might disappear, if he blinked he might find this had all been a cruel dream. Hope was for fools, yet he'd been a fool for this woman too many times to count. "What does that mean?"

Jennifer tightened her fingers, her heart beating a wild staccato rhythm against the wall of her chest. "I want to make love with you. I want to be your lover. I've wanted both for as long as I can remember."

She released her death grip on the post and crossed back to him. Cupping his face with her hands, she brushed her thumbs across his lips. "Say yes, Ryder. Say you'll be my lover."

Her words twisted in his gut, and he caught her hands. "I've long ago outgrown sex for sex's sake. That it would be good between us isn't enough, Jen. We have too much history to play these kinds of games. Find another stud."

She felt as if he'd slapped her, but she didn't cry out or move away. She inched her chin up, letting anger take her instead. "Damn you, Ryder. You have no idea what it cost me to come here today, no idea what the toll was for me to say what I did. You hold everyone accountable to your own narrow standards of honesty."

She swiped at the tears that squeezed from her eyes despite her vow not to cry. "Well, I'm not as bold as you are, I'm not as sure of myself and my feelings."

"Jennifer—"

He held out a hand, she slapped at it. "I was seventeen when we began dating, hardly old enough to understand what was happening between us, let alone deal with it. I can't even deal with it now at almost thirty." She drew in a deep, shuddering breath. "I'm sorry I didn't do everything right, and I'm sorry I hurt you. But you made mistakes, too, Ryder. You hurt me."

He took a step toward her, and she shook her head. "I never thought of this as a game, I never played with you. How could I? Everything I felt with you I always felt to the quick."

She crossed to the bed and collected her things. "You were right, we do have too much history for this." She shoved the brown-wrapped package into his hands as she brushed past him. "Here, I saved this for you."

As the door clicked shut behind her, Ryder peeled the paper away. Nestled inside was a piece of his past. A symbol of his independence, his defiance—the jacket he had worn everywhere.

Ryder rubbed the old, worn denim between his fingers, a smile pulling at the corners of his mouth. He'd loved this jacket. It had been as much a part of who he'd been back then as both Hazelhurst and being Sonny Keighton's best friend had been.

And Jennifer had kept it all these years. For him. Because of how she felt for him. His heart turned over. It would have been so easy for her to toss it—if she hadn't cared, if he hadn't meant anything to her.

He slipped the jacket on, the memory of that night at her window washing over him. She'd been so beautiful, so young. And he'd been so eager, so much in love.

She was right—they'd been too young back then for what had been burgeoning between them. So they had made mistakes, they had hurt each other. Both of them.

He went to the door, hoping he might catch her before she left the hotel. She hadn't even left the floor. She stood just beyond his door, partially behind a huge potted plant, blowing her nose. Tenderness and regret swelled inside him. "Jen."

She looked at him, her eyes red rimmed and wet, her face streaked with tears. "Go away."

"Ah, Jen..." He crossed to her and took her into his arms. "You make me feel too much. You always have."

She rubbed her face against his shoulder. "And you me."

He buried his face in her hair, drawing in her lovely scent. "Don't go."

She tipped her head back to meet his gaze. "I can't change the past, Ryder. We can't change history."

"No." He caught a tear that trembled on her lashes with his forefinger. "But maybe we shouldn't try. Maybe we should forget the past and try to start anew."

Start over. Jennifer curled her fingers into the soft weave of his T-shirt, her world righting, her heart mending. She'd trusted her instincts once before when it had come to Ryder and she'd been hurt . . . but that was part of the past. The time *had* come to begin anew.

"Where—" she drew a deep breath "—how do we begin?"

"Like this . . ." He pressed his lips to her eyebrows, her forehead, her wet cheeks. As he did, he combed his fingers through her hair, enjoying the way the coppery strands slipped around and through his fingers.

"And this," he whispered, lowering his mouth to hers.

He didn't press as she'd expected him to, didn't try to claim or possess. Instead his lips brushed exquisitely and ever so softly against hers, again and again.

Finally, with a sound of impatience, she lifted her hands to his hair and deepened the kiss.

He didn't deny her. Their lips parted, their tongues met and twined. She tightened her fingers in his thick, dark hair, wanting to deepen the kiss even more.

When that meeting could go no deeper, she moved against him in invitation.

"Jen—" he smiled against her lips "—we're out in the hall."

She felt the curving of his lips and returned it. "I told you once before," she murmured, nipping at his lower lip, "you touch me and I forget where I am. Besides, I don't care what people think."

"Well, I do." Ryder slid his hands down her back until they cupped underneath her, then he lifted.

Jennifer slid with excruciating slowness up his body, until her pelvis met the hardness of his. She hooked her legs around his waist.

"When it comes to you," he whispered against her lips, "I care very much what they think. Come."

He carried her to his room, closed and locked the door behind them. "It's going to be good, Jen. So good."

She laughed huskily. "I suddenly feel as fluttery as a schoolgirl."

"You don't feel like a schoolgirl to me." He lowered her as slowly as he'd lifted her, reveling in every second of the contact. "You feel like a woman. My woman."

Her pulse began to throb deeply, steadily, and she felt every inch the woman he'd called her.

And she *was* his. He had no idea how completely he already possessed her.

She ran her hands up and down his arms, then smoothed them over his shoulders. "I slept with this jacket once."

"It smells like you."

She pressed her face against his shoulder. "No. It smells like you."

He smiled. "I need a shower."

"No." She brought his mouth to hers once more. His trembled under hers, and she knew how great his need was for her. The knowledge thrilled her, made her daring. She leaned against him. "You smell clean—like exercise and fresh air.

"And you taste..." She pushed the jacket from his shoulders, then dragged her tongue along the side of his neck. Salt tingled against her tongue, and she imagined him as she'd first seen him today, breathless from his run, heart pounding and dripping with sweat. She wanted to make him that way without his moving a muscle.

"Shower with me." He laced his fingers with hers and led her to the bathroom.

While the water warmed, he stripped her of her shorts and shirt, then she of his. Not speaking, they stepped under the spray. The water sluiced over them, warming already heated flesh, slickening places that needed no moisture.

Jennifer soaped up her hands and slowly, lovingly, ran them over his body. Each muscle was a mystery and a delight, each breath he drew a pleasure beyond words.

Finally, she thought. She'd waited so long to be with this man. So long. Jennifer brazenly wandered her hands over him. She wanted to learn and explore, she wanted to taste and to savor. They knew each other in many ways, on so many intimate levels.

Now she would know him this way. As a lover. She would know his body, wonderful and hard and male. She would learn everything about it, from the scents of places not often kissed by the sun, to the texture of those same places, to the things that would arouse him beyond reason.

She found such a place with her fingers and she tested. He made a sound of pleasure. She found the place again, this time with her lips and tongue, and he cried out his approval.

Ryder caught her hands and brought them to his mouth. ''My turn,'' he whispered, taking the soap and lathering his own hands.

He moved them over her, taking his time, enjoying everything about being with her. He'd known he would. This was the only woman he had ever wanted. And now she was here with him, the way he'd fantasized her being—totally his.

He shuddered. A small part of him still feared it was all a dream, feared that if he moved the wrong way she would disappear.

But she wasn't disappearing and it wasn't a dream. She was warm and alive and wanting in his arms. She felt like silk and satin, she tasted like champagne and cream. She was everything he'd ever dreamed of, everything he'd thought too rich, too fine for a boy from The Creek.

He slid his hands over her, over the swells of perfect breasts, the slight curve of her abdomen, the indentation of her navel. Then lower to crisp hair and slick, warm flesh. He sank into her and she arched her back and cried out, clamping her legs together. He caught her mouth then, coaxed and stroked until, with a whimper, she opened herself to him.

He found her with his mouth then, and Jennifer flattened her hands against the wall of the shower, bracing herself. Her head fell back as the shock waves rolled over and through her. When she could stand no more, she curled her fingers into his hair and begged for release.

Ryder cut off the shower, and they stepped from the tub. There was a bed only a few feet away, neither could be bothered with it, just as they couldn't be bothered with towels. They sank to the floor, unable to wait another moment.

The cool air stung wet flesh, but where flesh pressed to flesh the heat was almost unbearable. Their tongues met and twined, and they laced their fingers. He sank into her.

He whispered her name, she answered with a kiss. She pleaded, he responded in a way that only created another, stronger plea. A sigh, a murmur; Jennifer arched her back and urged without sound.

The time for exploring and savoring passed, too immediate now was their need for either of those. Jennifer clutched at him, as he clutched at her. She wrapped her legs around him, holding, possessing.

I love you. The words filtered through her head, mixing with and around her passion. But when she opened her mouth to say them, the words wouldn't come. Instead a sound of her—their—passion came from her, and Ryder caught it with his mouth, making one of his own.

Release was brief but shattering, then it was over. Jennifer tumbled back to earth, back to reality, with him. And when she arrived she found, surprisingly, that she liked it. She felt neither awkward nor embarrassed nor worried. They knew each other too well for any of those.

Instead, when she looked up into his eyes, she felt contentment, real and poet perfect. She trailed a finger along his hard jaw. And she'd never felt this way before.

"What are you thinking?" she asked softly.

Ryder smiled down at her. "I was wondering if we'd ever get around to making love on a bed."

She returned his smile. "I guess I was a little impatient."

He laughed and arched his brows. "'A little impatient?' A kid standing in line to see Santa is a little impatient. A hungry construction worker waiting for the lunch whistle is a little impatient. A—"

Jennifer dragged his mouth to hers, silencing him. When she ended the kiss, his eyes had darkened to royal blue. She scowled playfully. "Was that what you were really thinking?"

"Uh-uh." He propped himself up on an elbow and moved his gaze slowly over her. "I was thinking you were the most beautiful woman in the world and the best thing that ever happened to me." He let the fingers of his right hand follow the path his eyes just had. "I was wondering how I could have thought for a single moment about letting you walk out that door. And—" he paused, enjoying the effect both his words and fingers were having on her "—I was thinking about cheeseburgers."

It took a moment for his last words to register. When they did, she let her breath out in an exaggerated huff. "Cheeseburgers!"

"Mmm-hmm. Big juicy ones, maybe even with bacon." He wiggled his brows. "Hungry?"

She laughed. "Starved!"

"Room service?"

"Anything else and I'd have to get out of bed."

"We're not in bed."

"I can remedy that."

"Vixen!"

She grinned. "You hope."

"What else should I order?"

"I don't care," she answered, stretching sinuously, knowing that he would follow the movement with his eyes, loving the appreciation, the heat, she saw in them. "As long as it's something really fattening. Something I wouldn't get caught dead eating in public, especially around other women."

Ryder stood, met her eyes and grinned. "I live to please."

"Yeah?"

"Yeah." He wiggled his eyebrows. "Last one to the bed gets a hickey that'll show."

With a squeal, Jennifer jumped up and raced after him.

Chapter Ten

Ryder ordered cheeseburgers, with fries on the side and hot fudge sundaes for dessert. Jennifer sat cross-legged on the huge four-poster bed, wearing nothing more than Ryder's denim jacket.

She tapped her finger thoughtfully against her chin as Ryder parked the cart by the bed. "You know, if we're really going to be bad, we should eat the sundaes first."

"You think so?" He cocked an eyebrow, amused. This was the Jennifer he remembered from high school, fun loving, a high-spirited practical joker, the girl who was always in a good mood, always ready for fun.

"I do." She pushed the tangle of hair away from her face. "Besides, won't the ice cream melt if we wait?"

"It will."

"See?" She reached around him and dunked her finger into the whipped cream. She brought it to her mouth and sucked it slowly off. "Mmm."

Arousal hit him with the force of a freight train traveling at high speed. "Jen," he warned softly, "you'd better be careful."

"Careful?" she repeated innocently, dipping the finger in again.

She leaned forward and the jacket parted. His breath caught. If he had pictured her this way at eighteen, he might never have reached nineteen—he would have dropped dead on the spot. As it was, he wasn't sure he would ever breathe evenly again.

"Jen," he muttered once more, this time as she plucked the cherry from one of the sundaes and, holding it by the stem above her, arched her neck and sucked the cream off it.

"What?" She angled an all-too-innocent glance up at him through lowered lashes. "I'm just eating."

When had his Jennifer become a coquette? He kneeled on the bed beside her. "And earlier we were just bathing."

"I like my sweets."

"I see that." She reached around him to nab the other cherry; he beat her to it. "Come get it." He held it out to her, but when she made a move for it, he popped it into his mouth.

Laughing, she knocked him onto his back and straddled his chest. "Give it back, Ryder. I have dibs on both cherries." When he only arched his brows, she narrowed her eyes. "You've left me no recourse but to go after it."

"Make my day," he challenged around the fruit.

She pressed her mouth to his. She tasted of whipped cream, the cherry she'd already consumed and laughter. He wrapped his arms tightly around her and rolled them over. Once again in the dominant position, he passed her the cherry.

Jennifer sank her teeth into it, and the juices spilled into both their mouths. They sucked, sharing the sweet liquid until there was nothing left to do but devour the fruit itself.

"More," Jennifer murmured against his lips, unwilling to let him go.

Ryder drew a fraction away from her. "There is no more. You ate both."

"I ate both?" She arched her brows indignantly.

He grinned. "Oink, oink, Jen."

She pinched him. "Call room service."

"I won't." He sat up, bringing her with him so she cuddled in his lap. "What would they think in the kitchen when they got the order for a bowlful of maraschino cherries?"

Jennifer nibbled at his ear. "Don't care."

"Right."

She tipped her head back. "Boy, the things you learn about a guy...you're so disagreeable."

"And you—" he slipped his hands under the denim jacket and ran his hands over her silky skin "—are so bad."

"And if you're going to be so disagreeable," she continued, lifting her eyes to his, her lips curving into a slow, wicked smile, "I'll just have to find a way to make you do my bidding."

"What do you have in mind?"

She roamed her hands over him. "I'll show you."

And she did.

Sunlight streamed across the bed. Jennifer opened her eyes slowly, becoming aware of several things simultaneously—the scent of sex that lingered on the sheets, the sweet ache in parts of her body that had never ached before, the deep, welcoming cadence of Ryder's breathing.

It was the last she liked best, and Jennifer propped herself up on an elbow, careful not to awaken him. She wanted these moments to gaze at him, to absorb and memorize everything about him—from the tiny scar above his right eyebrow to the way, even relaxed as he was, one corner of his mouth lifted in a naughty little smirk.

He was so beautiful. Not in the traditional smooth, suave sense. But wickedly so. Darkly so. She moved her gaze over him. Even in sleep he looked like the bad boy—wicked, dangerous...totally irresistible.

She shook her head. How could someone who looked like that be as gentle as he was? And how could a boy—now a man—who had endured so much cruelty know so much about tenderness?

She shuddered, remembering the last time they'd made love. He had awakened her with feather-light strokes, his hard hands capable of caresses of unbelievable tenderness. He had coaxed with words as well, saying things no one had ever said to her before, taking her places she hadn't even dared imagine.

Unable to help herself, she trailed a finger along his shadowed jaw, then along the arch of one of his dark brows. He wiggled his nose and she giggled, then slapped a hand over her mouth to catch another.

He stirred, shifted, but didn't open his eyes. She reached out to touch him again, and he growled. The sound came from low in his throat and was meant to be menacing but it didn't scare her in the least, and she ran her hands over him anyway.

"You're awake," she teased.

"Go away," he said, his voice a just-awakened, sexy rasp.

"No." She sat up in bed, pulling the covers with her. As she did, they slipped off Ryder in several key locations.

He partially lifted his lids and met her eyes. "I'm not a morning person, Jennifer. I'm coyote-mean until about noon, and I only growl until I've had several cups of strong coffee. Consider yourself warned." He tugged on the blankets. "Go away."

Jennifer laughed, leaned over and blew in his ear. "Well, I am a morning person. Up with the sun is my motto."

"Why aren't I surprised?"

His tone dripped sarcasm, she let it pass anyway. She leaned her elbows onto his chest, resting her chin on her folded hands. "What do you want to do today?"

He pulled the pillow over his face.

She peeked underneath. "Today *is* Sunday. I think we should go to church. Especially after last night."

Ryder smiled, she suspected he couldn't help himself.

"Plus," she continued, not missing a beat, "I have an open house at three, that means I'll have to start putting out the signs about two-thirty. The day will be gone before we know it."

Ryder tipped the pillow up and looked at her. "Is that a problem?"

"Be serious."

"What about food?"

She laughed. "It's always the same with you—food and sex, food and sex."

Ryder growled again. This time the sound had nothing to do with either annoyance or sleep. "Now that you've reminded me...."

"Oh, no..." She slipped out of the bed and started for the bathroom. "Service is at nine sharp, and I intend to be there. And don't forget, I still have to stop at home for clothes and makeup."

Ryder sat up, tossing the pillow to the floor. "You're serious about this, aren't you?"

"And I want to go to the Short Stack after. For pancakes."

"Pancakes?" he repeated doubtfully. "At the Short Stack?"

"That's what I said."

"You do remember that Sunday mornings at the Stack is Hazelhurst's closest equivalent to Grand Central Station?"

Ignoring his question, Jennifer looked back at him from the doorway of the bathroom. "And by my calculations, if you get up now and we shower together, we'll have a bit of time for... other things."

She flashed him her most provocative smile, then shut the door behind her.

"You don't have to do this," Ryder said an hour and twenty-three minutes later as they pulled into the lot adjacent to the Hazelhurst Episcopalian church.

Jennifer looked at at the old-fashioned white-frame structure. The steeple jutted into the sky and she remembered gazing up at it as a child and feeling totally awed.

"I like church," Jennifer said quietly, nervously smoothing an imaginary wrinkle from her turquoise-colored linen skirt.

"That's not what I meant, and you know it." Ryder covered her hand with his. "You don't have to test yourself, not for me anyway."

She gazed at him, a trembling sensation in the pit of her stomach. For a fraction of a second she almost gave in to the feeling and called the whole thing off. Her parents would be in there, their friends as well as hers, people who knew them both from the past.

And she wouldn't have to explain what she was doing with Ryder, everyone would know.

Drawing a deep breath, Jennifer straightened her spine. The time had come to stop worrying about appearances and what her parents wanted for her and to start following her heart.

She squeezed his hand. "No, I do have to do it." She leaned over and brushed her lips against his. "Thanks for the out anyway."

Her parents were there, as she'd known they would be, standing just inside the door and talking to their bridge partners of the past twenty years.

Jennifer pasted a smile on her face. "Mom, Dad?"

Her parents turned to her, their smiled fading as they saw who she was with. They both opened their mouths as if to say something, but nothing came out.

After an awkward moment, the other woman smiled. "Jennifer, honey, you look wonderful. You always do, but today you look particularly so. Vibrant even," she added, sliding her gaze to Ryder.

"Thanks, Mrs. Dix." Jennifer caught Ryder's hand. "Do you know Ryder Hayes?"

Both she and her husband gracefully admitted remembering him, and the conversation went on from there, although her parents never did manage to get a word out. Through the whole ordeal, Ryder kept a reassuring hand on her elbow, seeming unaffected by the awkwardness of the conversation or the tension emanating from her parents in palpable waves.

She wished she could say the same about herself. The longer her parents remained silent, the more disappointed—distraught even—they looked, the more the trembling sensation in her middle spread. By the time the organist began to play the introductory hymn, her voice was quavering and her knees knocking.

From the service she and Ryder went to the Short Stack, and once again her parents were there. And once again Jennifer joined them without invitation.

Only this time there were no old family friends with whom to make conversation. Her father sat ramrod straight in the booth, his face flushed, his features set in hard, angry lines. And if looks could have killed, Ryder wouldn't have lived long enough to order, and she would no doubt have ended up walking with a permanent limp.

After a few minutes of strained silence, her mother began to chatter. "Wonderful sermon today, didn't you think?"

"Yes," Jennifer responded, relieved to finally have the ice broken. "There seemed to be a fuller congregation today as well."

"It should be an excellent collection plate."

"Mmm." Jennifer searched for something to add, but all she could think of was the way Ryder and her father were glaring at each other and the squeak of strain in her mother's voice.

After several moments, her mother began again, "It's supposed to be warmer next week. But frankly, I don't see how. It's already been miserable."

"I heard that, too." Jennifer peeked at Ryder from the corners of her eyes. He seemed to be growing stiffer, his mood darker, by the second. "I'll be happy to see fall."

Her mother took a sip of her coffee, then patted her mouth with a napkin. "I say that every August first."

Their breakfasts came then and even though she drenched her pancakes in the rich, buttery syrup, Jennifer couldn't eat more than a couple of bites.

No one else at the table seemed any more interested in food than she, and it wasn't long before they all gave up the pretense and pushed their plates away.

As if on cue, the waitress rushed to the table and deposited the check. Both Ryder and her father grabbed it. Their eyes met, seconds ticked past. Neither relinquished his hold on the paper.

"I've got it, Hayes."

Ryder tightened his fingers. "No, Henry, I've got it."

Her father's flush deepened and he narrowed his eyes. "I insist."

"Do you?" Ryder stared at the older man for what seemed an eternity, then just as Jennifer's heart began to throb in earnest, he dropped his hand. "Well, if that's the case."

"It is."

"Fine."

The silence that had enveloped the table continued as they walked out of the restaurant. And as before, her mother broke it. "I wish you all had decided to have your reunion in the fall." She fanned herself. "It would have been so much prettier, and I believe you might have had an even greater turn... oh, dear, I almost forgot."

Jennifer dragged her thoughts back to her mother. "Forgot what, Mom?"

"I meant to tell you at church, but when you... I mean, with all the excitement..." She reached for her purse and drew out a small cream-colored envelope. "This came for you."

"For me?" Jennifer took it, her fingers trembling. The paper was of the highest quality, with the return information embossed on the back flap. California. She only knew one person there.

"It's from Cyndi," her mother said unnecessarily but obviously too excited to wait for Jennifer's response. "I bet I know why she's writing."

Jennifer drew a deep breath, then carefully opened the envelope. The note read:

Dearest Jennifer,
So much time has passed I hardly know how or where to begin. There is much I want to say to you, much I need to explain. I hope you'll allow me the opportunity to do so when I come home for our tenth reunion. I can hardly wait to see you again.

Yours, Cyndi

Jennifer closed her fingers around the card and stared blankly at her mother, then shifted her gaze to Ryder's. "Cyndi's coming home. She's coming to the reunion."

Her mother clasped her hands together. "I knew it!"

"I can't believe she's coming back," Jennifer murmured, still looking at Ryder. "After all these years."

"We'll shop for that new dress tomorrow. You'll want to look your best for your old friends."

"What?" Jennifer turned back to her mother at the use of the plural.

"Meredith's coming too. Her mother told me yesterday. I tried to call you all day and well into the evening but—" the older woman's cheeks pinkened and she seemed to avoid looking at anyone "—I couldn't reach you."

Jennifer lowered her eyes to the envelope clutched in her hand. After all these years, she would see her old friends again. What would they think of who she'd become? Would they be surprised? Disappointed? Or wouldn't it matter to them at all?

"...should call her father..."

Cyndi. Meredith. Ryder. Herself. All the old group but one. All but Sonny.

"...told me Meredith is newly married. I can't remember when she said the wedding was held..."

Jennifer caught her lower lip between her teeth as a dozen different emotions collided within her, not the least of which was guilt. Sonny had died. And she could have prevented it if only—

"Jen? Are you okay?"

At the question she turned toward Ryder. She drew her eyebrows together, looking at him as if she were seeing him for the first time.

What would her old friends think of her and Ryder together?

"Jen?"

She blinked. "What?"

"Are you okay?"

She shook her head. "I'm fine. Just ready to go home."

"Right," Ryder muttered, and without another word, started for the car.

He didn't speak again until he'd stopped the car in front of her house. "Great Sunday, Jen. Wonderful suggestion."

She turned to him, surprised by the anger in his voice. "Where did that come from?"

"Take a wild guess."

Her carefully constructed calm shattered, and she glared at him. "If you're going to be a part of my life, you're going to have to be a part of my parents' lives and vice versa."

He returned her icy gaze. "We never had that problem before, did we? Oh, that's right, I wasn't really a part of your life back then."

Tears sprang to her eyes. Furious, Jennifer blinked them away. "We agreed the past would stay in the past. That was a cheap shot." She slammed out of the car and marched up the walk to her front door.

Ryder followed her. Inside, she turned on him. "You could have tried to make conversation. You could have at least been supportive."

"Supportive?" he repeated, equally furious. "I was there, wasn't I? And what would you have had me say? 'Sure, Henry, go ahead and take a punch?'"

"My father did not want to hit you."

"No, but he didn't have a gun, Jennifer." He yanked on his tie, loosening it. "Besides, I didn't hear you doing too much talking."

"I talked!"

"About the weather, for Pete's sake. Come on."

She angled her chin up. "What would you have had me say?"

"If you don't know, then this thing is even more ridiculous than I thought."

The tears were back, choking her words. "Why are you so angry with me?"

"I don't like being forced down people's throats."
He tossed the tie onto a chair. "I don't like it and I
won't stand for it. Not again."

"They're my parents. I want them to accept you."

"If that's a prerequisite for this relationship, we
better pack it in now." He shrugged out of his jacket,
then turned and met her eyes. "Well?"

She stared at him, eyes swimming. "Dammit, Ryder, I didn't mean for today to hurt you. I only
meant...only wanted..." She shook her head, her
words trailing off.

He muttered a short, blunt word and dragged his
hands through his hair. "I'm not angry at you. I'm
angry at the whole thing—that my old man was a
worthless drunk, that you had to go through what you
did this morning, that Sonny died.

"And I'm tired, Jen. Tired of having to fight the
world, tired of having to fight for you. It seems I've
been doing it forever, starting way back with Sonny."

"Sonny?"

"Yeah, your precious golden boy. I came back for
you that night, prom night. That's when I met
Sonny." He shook his head and reached for his jacket.
"Forget it."

"No, I don't want to forget it." She tossed her head
back. "I don't think you do, either."

"You want to hear what happened that night?" he
asked roughly, catching her hands, his grip as hard as
the expression in his eyes. "The ungarnished truth?
Whatever it is?"

"Yes." She jerked her chin up again. "The truth."

Ryder set her away from him, then crossed to the window. Sunlight spilled through the panes of glass, drenching him in light. The day seemed too brilliant, Jennifer thought sadly, too clear, for remembering a past so colored with darkness. And for the words they seemed unable to stop flinging at each other.

"I wanted that night to be perfect for you," he began quietly. "I'd become almost obsessed by the want. I knew I was your second choice. I wanted to make up for that, maybe even prove to you I was good enough to be number one."

"Oh, Ryder. I—"

"No, Jennifer. Let me finish." He leaned against the window casing, continuing to gaze out at the day. "The night didn't start out so great, first a fight with my old man, then yours warned me that if I so much as inched out of line he'd kill me. Then that nightmare of a dinner..."

Ryder laughed a little and touched one of the old-fashioned lace curtains. "Still, being with you was enough. You looked so beautiful—" he met her eyes over his shoulder "—I remember the exact shade of your gown, how the fabric whispered when you moved...how it felt beneath my hands. Lord knows, I wished I didn't."

He shook his head and looked away once more. "I was young and wildly in love, ridiculously hopeful. I still thought love had some magical power, that it could somehow transcend all obstacles. Grand romantic thoughts from a boy who had never known anything but ugliness. But maybe those thoughts were all I had to keep me from the sewer myself."

Jennifer's eyes filled with tears and she fought them back, them and a sound of pain. She wrapped her arms around herself and waited.

"Then in came Sonny," Ryder continued, his tone grim. "My buddy. My best friend." He laughed without humor. "He must have known that something was going on between us, must have sensed that I was going to make my move."

Ryder shrugged. "Whatever, he made it clear you were his property and that I had better keep off his turf. He even laughed at the notion that someone like you would want a punk like me.

"Until that moment, I'd thought Sonny was my friend. Then I saw it all very clearly. I was never really his friend—he'd used me as a kind of alter ego. Through me he did all the things he was afraid to do. And as he'd lent you to me, he lent himself, his Sonny-stature. He thought he was doing me a hell of a favor. Does that make sense?"

Ryder didn't expect an answer, and Jennifer didn't give him one. "I was furious, hurt. I felt betrayed. I told him he had a girl and to take a flying leap. That's when he told me—" Ryder turned and met her eyes "—that you and he had met earlier."

"Met earlier?" Jennifer repeated, drawing her eyebrows together. "What do you mean?"

"After dinner, while you were supposedly taking care of prom stuff, while Cyndi was powdering her nose for the billionth time. He said you'd sneaked away to plan how you would be together, that you'd kissed. It was the final blow."

So, that's why Ryder had been so cold, so angry with her at the dance. And that's why he and Sonny had been so near tearing each other apart.

Over her. And over a lie.

Jennifer worked to control her breathing. "I didn't," she murmured, overwhelmed. "You have to believe me. I didn't see Sonny until we got to the table."

"I'm not sure it matters anymore."

A sob caught in her throat. "It does matter. A lie always matters. If you don't believe me, it'll always be between us."

"Like another lie, Jen?" he returned softly. "Shall we trade one for one?"

"One for—"

"Did I tell Sonny we were doing it?" When she only stared at him, he crossed to her, cupped her face in his palms and stared deeply into her eyes. "Yes or no, Jennifer. Did I or didn't I?"

Jennifer met his gaze, her heart beating slowly, heavily against the wall of her chest. She thought of that night, of Sonny and Ryder. She thought of the nights before and since.

Relief, sweet and healing, flowed through her. She'd known the truth since he'd come to her house and they'd consummated their passion. Maybe even longer.

"Sonny lied," she said evenly. "You would never· have betrayed me the way he said you did."

Ryder tightened his fingers as he searched her eyes. A moment later, he dropped his hands and turned away from her.

Heat stung her cheeks. He didn't believe her! She caught his arm and swung him back around. "You let me down. That night in the garden, I wanted to make love, but I was terrified of becoming pregnant. I was a virgin, Ryder! But instead of soothing me, reassuring me, you walked away."

"Isn't the truth more that you worried about telling your parents—everyone, really—that you were pregnant by me?"

"No!" Even as the word passed her lips, doubt set in. All these years she'd thought Ryder had coldly abandoned her, but now...she wasn't sure what she believed. His words had a ring of truth and yet...

She couldn't go back to eighteen, couldn't go back to that night to know the absolute truth. The ten years between then and now might as well be a century. Memories had become skewed, real feelings had been obscured by time and rationalizations.

"And that same night," he went on, "if I'd told you how I felt and asked you if there was a chance for us, what would you have told me?"

She wet her suddenly parched lips. "I don't know...it's been years and..." She shook her head. "I just don't know."

Ryder slipped his hands into his pockets and moved restlessly around the room. He paused at the picture-lined mantel, staring at the rows of photos for a moment before turning back to her. "I love you, Jen. I always have. I couldn't admit that even a week ago, but now I see there's no escaping it."

He glanced back at the pictures. "Love's easy. It comes, it happens, free will is snatched away by the heart. But trust—'' he lowered his voice ''—trust is hard. It's conscious, it's choice. I trusted once with everything I had, and I was almost destroyed. I don't know if I can ever take that step again.''

His words were like a blow to her chest. One moment she'd had his love, the next it was tainted by regret. By doubt.

And underlying the words, his message was clear—this is the best it's going to get, take it or leave it.

Eyes brimming with tears, she said, ''What happened that night, Ryder? How did you and Sonny end up on the bike?''

He told her. About his words with Sonny in front of the gymnasium. About the accident.

And when he'd finished, Jennifer sank to the edge of the couch, drained from reliving the night with him. And from reliving each of her own emotions.

She dropped her head into her hands, struggling for control, struggling with the hurt that welled inside of her until she thought she might burst from it. Lips trembling, she looked up at him. ''I lost everybody that night.''

''We both did.''

''I love you,'' she whispered. At his expression she laughed hollowly. ''See, you don't have the corner on fear. I knew I loved you when I came to you yesterday, but I was too terrified to tell you. You could have rejected me. You almost did.''

He crossed to her, caught her hands and drew her to her feet. ''Only because you were acting like the only thing you were interested in was sex. I needed it—us—to be important.''

"How could you have doubted it? I had my heart pinned to my sleeve."

"Under layers and layers of fabric." He tangled his fingers in her hair. "You need a tissue."

"Always these days." She sniffed. "How did everything get so screwed up?"

"I don't know." A hint of a smile curved his mouth. "Talent, I guess."

"What are we going to do now?"

"I've got some ideas. And none of them include talking." He swung her into his arms and carried her to the stairs.

Chapter Eleven

"You're humming again."

At Susan's murmured comment, Jennifer looked up. Her partner stood in the doorway, her expression enigmatic. "Pardon?"

"You're humming again. You've been doing it for a week now."

Jennifer thought of Ryder, and a small smile curved her mouth. "Have I?"

"Yes." Susan sauntered into the office. "It's driving me crazy."

"I never could carry a tune."

"That's not it." Susan slumped into the chair across from hers. "It's all the good cheer that's making me nuts."

Jennifer grinned. Even her parents' sour mood couldn't dim hers. She and Ryder had spent a wonderful, delicious, fulfilling week together. The week had passed without one unhappy argument, without one ounce of sludge dredged up from their past.

And as each day had gone by, she'd been able to shove her doubts further aside until she almost believed they really could pull this thing off.

"I'll try to be more sullen, Susan. Really, I will."

"Promises, promises..."

Jennifer laughed. "It's not that bad. Look—" she waved the offer that had just come in on one of her priciest properties, under Susan's nose "—a real live offer! One that my client has already accepted. This proves it, there are buyers out there. All we have to do is wait them out."

"That's not what's bothering me."

Jennifer lifted her eyebrows in surprise. Business was what was always bothering Susan.

The other woman sighed and picked up one of the many framed photos of Jennifer's niece and nephew that she had scattered over the top of her desk. Susan studied it a moment, a strange expression on her face, then set it back down. "So, does your humming of late have anything to do with a certain old friend?"

"Could be."

"Hmm." Susan arched an eyebrow. "What about his house hunting?"

"At a standstill." Jennifer's smile slipped just a bit. "I don't think he'll be staying long enough to lease anything."

Susan tapped a perfectly manicured nail on the arm of the chair. "He probably trumped up the whole house thing just to get you to spend time with him."

"Probably."

"I like a man who has initiative." Susan tapped the finger again. "If he's not staying, where does that leave you?"

"I don't know," Jennifer answered, surprising herself. This was as candid—and as personal—as she and Susan had ever gotten. "He hasn't mentioned the future."

"The future," the other woman repeated absently, a faraway look in her eyes.

Jennifer cocked her head. Something was different about Susan this morning. Something—

She snapped her fingers, realizing what it was. "You're not smoking."

"I quit."

"You're kidding?"

"I'm pregnant."

Jennifer stared at her, stunned silent. One moment became two, became ten. "I'm sorry, I'm not sure I heard you correc—"

"You heard correctly. I'm going to have a baby. In March."

"That's wonderful!" Jennifer stood to go hug her, then suddenly self-conscious, straightened her skirt and sat back down. "I'm speechless."

"Now that is an accomplishment," the other woman muttered, her tone dry. "Drake's thrilled."

Jennifer's smile faded. "But how do *you* feel?"

"Besides nauseous?" Jennifer nodded. "Like an idiot."

Jennifer arched her eyebrows. "An idiot? I don't understand."

Susan squirmed in her seat. "I always said I didn't want kids...in fact I've been quite vocal about it with family, friends." She lowered her eyes to her hands, clasped in her lap. "And here I am, tickled pink and as giddy as a schoolgirl."

This time when Jennifer stood, she raced around the desk. The other woman stood also and they hugged each other.

"So much for the hard-bitten career lady, huh?"

Jennifer wiped the moisture on her friend's cheeks, laughing, knowing there were tears on her own, as well. She hugged her again, not wanting to let the other woman go. It had been a long time since she'd had a girlfriend to laugh and cry and share with. Too long. She thought of Meredith and Cyndi and her tears came harder.

"Hey? Are you all right?" Susan held her at arm's length.

"Just happy." Jennifer laughed and wiped at her tears. "I'm the one who's an idiot. It seems like all I do is cry these days."

"This have something to do with the guy?"

Jennifer shook her head, sniffing. "Not these tears."

Susan plucked a couple of tissues from the box on Jennifer's desk. She handed her one and kept the other for herself. "Want to talk about it?"

With a shock, Jennifer realized she did. "It's a long story."

Susan sat down again, making herself comfortable. "I have lots of time. Business is bad, remember?"

So Jennifer told her. About Cyndi and Meredith and Sonny. About the night of the prom and the events after. She focused on her friends, excluding all but the necessary details about Ryder—those still felt too personal, too private.

"Wow," Susan said as Jennifer finished and, drained, sank into a chair. "You sure know how to keep a pregnant lady from thinking about food." She leaned forward. "And you've never seen or heard from your friends again?"

"They're coming to the reunion. I just learned."

Susan whistled. "I hope you've bought one hell of a dress."

Jennifer laughed, appreciating Susan's dry wit more than ever. "You sound like my mother."

"That's because I'm going to be one." She patted her flat stomach proudly. "Do you know what you're going to say to these long-lost friends?"

"I haven't the faintest. And that scares me to death." Jennifer leaned her head against the chair back. "Any suggestions?"

"Punt."

Jennifer rolled her eyes. "Thanks."

"Any time." Susan stood and stretched, arching her back. "Keep me posted."

"I will." Smiling, Jennifer watched her business partner exit the office. She liked her, Jennifer realized. She liked her and they *were* friends. She'd always used their differences as an excuse for why she and Susan weren't close. But the truth was, the other woman had left the door open time and again for real friendship. And time and again Jennifer had shut the door, preferring to hold her at arm's length, afraid of being hurt.

Leaving the door open had felt good. Damn good. She'd have to try it again.

Humming, she leaned back in her chair. Her mother and Susan were right. She needed a knock-down gorgeous dress for the reunion. Not for her old friends—she grinned, not just for her old friends anyway—but for herself. She deserved to feel special for this special occasion.

Jennifer straightened in her chair, realizing this was the first time she'd thought of the reunion as special, the first time she'd felt any excitement about it. Instead, she'd spent the past year trudging through its preparations and wishing she could use the excuse of distance to avoid attending.

No more! Today she began anticipating instead of dreading. She flipped through her appointment book then snapped it shut. It appeared there was no time like the present to start.

Two and a half hours later, Jennifer dumped an arm load of packages into her back seat, including a dress bag bearing Sinclaire's name and logo.

She smiled and slipped into the driver's seat. She'd spent a lot more money than she should have. The pure silk lingerie had been an extravagance beyond her wildest dreams. Her cheeks heated as she not only thought of the teddy and stockings but pictured herself wearing them for Ryder.

Jennifer started the car. She'd gotten the raspberry-colored dress her mother had effused about two months ago after all. She checked her watch. Her book was clear until late afternoon, why not stop by and surprise her mother with both her purchases and an offer of lunch?

Why not, indeed. Singing softly, she headed for her parents' house.

Her father's car was parked in the driveway. He'd come home for lunch. Jennifer pulled in behind it, then stepped out of her own vehicle, collecting all her packages from the back seat.

She let herself into the house. "Mom, Dad, it's me."

She dropped her packages onto the couch, then headed for the kitchen. She stopped in her tracks when she reached it. Her father was sitting at the table, her mother stooped beside him, her arms around his shoulders, their heads pressed together.

Jennifer's heart leaped to her throat—something had happened to Christopher or one of the kids. Struggling to control her ragged breathing, she took another step into the room.

"Mom...Dad...what's happened?"

They both looked up. It was obvious by their expressions that they hadn't heard her call out. Her mother's eyes were bloodshot and wet...and so were her father's.

Oh, God, Jennifer thought, panic tightening in her chest, please let the kids be okay. She placed a hand on the door frame for support. "Has there been an accident? Have one of the—"

"Your father was let go today," her mother said quietly.

"Let go," Jennifer repeated, her knees turning to jelly. "No, that...can't be."

"Put out to pasture, forced into retirement. Thirty years of service shot to..." He shook his head and let the words trail off.

The bitterness in her father's voice threw her. She'd never heard him sound quite like that, had never seen such disillusionment in his eyes. At that moment he seemed many years older than he was, many years older than he had been the other day. He looked like an old and broken man.

"How did they...when did it...happen?" she asked, her voice shaking.

"First thing this morning," her father muttered. "I didn't even get the courtesy of a call. They sent me a fax."

Then it couldn't have been Ryder who did it, Jennifer thought dizzily. Oh, please let it not have been him.

"Do you think you have any recourse, Henry?" her mother asked. "Do you think we could get a lawyer and—"

He shook his head. "I don't think so. They claim reorganization and economic conditions and a bunch of other crap that's hard to fight. And frankly, I don't think I have the energy."

Jennifer's heart turned over. "Can I see the letter, Dad?" He tossed it onto the table, and with trembling fingers, she picked it up and scanned the shockingly short correspondence. It came from Lansing's corporate headquarters. Neither Ryder nor the work he was doing at the plant were mentioned.

Relief flowed through her. "I'll talk to Ryder. Maybe he can—"

"Talk to him?" her father shot back at her. "This recommendation was his!"

Jennifer took a step back at the fury in his eyes. Never before had he looked at her like that. "But the letter doesn't—"

"Why else would they do this?" her father asked bitterly. "Everything was fine until he showed up."

Jennifer's hands began to shake. It couldn't be. Ryder hadn't mentioned the plant, hadn't mentioned anything about changes. She'd trusted him, she'd believed that he would do everything he could to save the plant and her father's job. Surely he would have said something to her.

"Dad," she said softly, "are you sure Ryder—"

"Even after this you're still going to defend that boy?" her mother demanded, turning on her. "We both tried to warn you about him. About his motives. What is it with you and him? Why is it so difficult for you to see what everyone else does?"

"Mom, I—"

Her mother held up a hand. "Just let me ask you this, Jennifer Marie—do you still think you know him? Do you still think he wouldn't do anything to hurt us?"

Tears flooded her eyes, and she wrapped her arms around herself. *Ryder had betrayed her. Again.*

"It seems," her father said, "I should have let him pay for breakfast after all."

"Oh, Dad—" the words were choked with tears "—I'm so sorry. Is there anything I can do?"

"Find me another job," he answered, looking up at his wife. "What am I going to do, Mary? Who's going to hire a fifty-six-year-old man?"

Her mother put her arms around him again and Jennifer stood there, shut out because she'd given her loyalty to someone other than her family, because, as she had ten years ago, she'd trusted Ryder. Guilt and shame, anger and remorse all warred within her.

Anger won.

Without taking the time to collect her things, she raced from her childhood home.

Ryder set the phone back in its cradle, drawing his eyebrows together in concern. He'd left a message for Jennifer on her machine at home. He'd called her office several times, and each time, the receptionist told him the same thing—she wasn't back yet, she had no idea where she was but would have her call the second she got in.

But the second she got in might be too late. It might be too late even now.

Ryder picked up the fax that had come just that morning and swore. When he had seen it, he'd thought there must have been some mistake. Headquarters had confirmed the opposite. The truth had hit him then— Henry had been forced out and Ryder'd been screwed.

He swore again and tossed the correspondence aside. Jennifer would be devastated. He wanted to talk to her, explain the situation, before she saw her father. Ryder checked his watch again. But with each second that ticked by, his apprehension that what he wanted wouldn't be a reality grew.

Ryder thought of Henry Joyce, of the look on his face as he'd burst into his office. His expression had been a mixture of disbelief, rage and bitterness. And Henry had caught him unawares—the corporation hadn't even seen fit to let him know in advance.

The older man blamed him for it all. That had been obvious. And understandable. It was so much easier to blame another than acknowledge what had really happened—the corporation had decided to phase him out.

But would Jennifer blame him, as well? He swiveled his chair around until he faced the window behind him. If her love was worth having, she would believe in him, he thought fiercely. If there was any kind of a chance for them she would stand by him.

"How could you do this?"

At Jennifer's softly spoken question, he slowly turned the chair back around. One look at her expression and both his questions were answered. He *was* too late. And she did think him responsible. In that moment it felt as if something exquisite and bright, something necessary to living, had been snatched from him.

"How could you?" she repeated. "He's my father."

The cold in her eyes clawed at him. He'd never dreamed she could look at him like that. Especially after their past week together. "Come in and sit down. We need to talk."

"Go to hell!" She took a step back. "Just tell me how, after what we've shared, you could do this?"

"I didn't do it, Jen. That's just it. The corporation—"

She laughed, the sound hard and unforgiving. "I read the letter, Ryder."

"The order didn't come from me."

"No," she said scathingly, "just from your recommendation." Tears filled her eyes and she shook her head, denying them. "He's fifty-six years old, Ryder. You know how hard it's going to be for him to find another position. And even if he does, it won't be anywhere near the caliber of the one he has now. Had," she corrected, choking on the word. "Why didn't you say something?"

Ryder stood and came around the desk. "I tried to call you this morning. You'll find messages—"

"This morning? After the deed was done?"

"I only learned this morning myself." He took another step toward her. "I know you're upset. I don't blame you. But this isn't what it seems. If you'd just take a deep breath and—"

"You know, Ryder, it's always 'not what it seems' with you, isn't it? Or maybe more, it is what it seems to everyone but poor, blind Jennifer." She whirled away from him, dragging her hands through her hair. "God, I've been such an idiot."

She looked back at him. "I trusted you. Twice now. I believed in you, in your word. I defended you to everyone...to my parents." She wrapped her arms around herself, fighting back the pain, focusing on her anger. "And both times you tossed that trust back in my face."

Her words hurled him back ten years, to an antiseptic hospital room and words that had changed his life forever. But he wasn't eighteen anymore, and he'd worked too hard and come too far to ever go back. "Is that what you believe, Jennifer?"

"I'll tell you what I *can't* believe—that I've been such a fool. Has everything been a lie? Everything you told me about the past, everything we've done together?" She took a step toward him, meeting his eyes evenly. "Was sleeping with me just another part of your plan for revenge?"

Her words hit him with the force of a wrecking ball. Nothing had changed: she'd convicted him without explanation let alone trial, just as she had ten years before.

Pain slammed into him. Even though he'd vowed not to trust, even though he'd convinced himself he'd never again give anyone the power to destroy him, it felt as if he were dying inside.

"Sleeping with you for revenge?" he repeated icily. "Appearances would suggest the opposite."

She tossed her head back. "Excuse me?"

"Perhaps you slept with me to secure your father's job."

"Bastard!"

She raised a hand to slap him, but he caught it. "Doesn't feel so great, does it, Jen?"

When she tried to free her hand, he caught her other wrist. "Ten years ago I didn't defend myself. To you or anyone else. I was too proud. So instead I slunk out of town as if I really had done something wrong."

"Let me go." She tugged against his grasp; he only tightened his fingers.

"I realized my mistake too late, but I promised myself I'd never make the same one again." He shook her a little, forcing her to look at him. "You're going to listen to me, Jen. Not that I care anymore what you think, but because this time I'm not leaving without defending myself.

"I've worked damn hard to save this plant and all its jobs—including your father's. I did it because I care about this town and the people who live here. But am I going to be a hero?" Ryder laughed bitterly. "No, I'm the same punk kid that was run out on a rail ten years ago."

Jennifer stared up at him, a fluttering in the pit of her stomach. She caught her lower lip between her teeth to keep it from trembling. His eyes were brilliant with fury—and yet something in them reminded her of that bruised boy of ten years before.

Hurt. Accusation.

Oh, dear God, she thought. Had she made a mistake? Had she—

"I pulled a rabbit out of the hat for Hazelhurst. Any other controller would have closed the plant down. But I didn't want to do that. So I worked with the union and the corporation and the figures. I made cuts, adjustments. And when that still wasn't good enough for headquarters, I convinced the men and the union to agree to a wage cut in exchange for some added benefits and programs."

The fluttering became breathlessness. Jennifer sucked in air to steady herself, but it had the opposite effect.

"As for your father, his techniques are outdated and he has the most inflated salary on the payroll. But still, because of you and because of his age, I recommended he stay."

"But he was let go," she said weakly. "He—"

"It seems corporate had their own agenda. They went behind my back. How do you like that, Jen? I've been punched in the gut twice today."

The tears she'd fought off earlier were back, only this time she didn't think she had the energy to stop them. "Why didn't you tell me? You haven't said a thing about any of this. If you had only told me, I wouldn't have thought that you...I wouldn't have..." Hearing how damning her own words were, she let them trail off.

He laughed, the sound hard and hollow against the backdrop of their breathing. "I wanted to surprise you with what a wonderful guy I was." He met her gaze. "Surprise."

"Oh, God." She pulled away from him, and this time he didn't resist letting her go. "I didn't know what to think...what to believe. You should have seen my father...my mother...the things they said about you. About my allegiance to you. It was awful, Ryder. I—"

"Don't lose any sleep, babe," he said coldly, and swung away from her. "You never believed in me before. Why start now?"

Her breath caught at the words. "Don't say that! I have believed in you."

"Not when it mattered." He looked over his shoulder at her. "Think about it. Even last weekend when we went to church, then breakfast, you never once told your parents how you felt about me. You say you defended me to them, but you never did.

"You sat there like a guilty child. I didn't realize it then, but I was angry because I wanted you to do both those things. I wanted you to stand by me, not feel tainted by association."

Jennifer folded her arms across her aching chest. If only she could go back, if only she could— She shook her head, fighting tears. The words couldn't be taken back, not ever.

"You said I didn't have to test myself for you. You said it didn't matter."

"You shouldn't have to test," he said softly. "Pride in another person, belief in them, trust—they should just be there, natural as breathing. They're not with us, they never will be. I've been a fool to hope they would magically spring out of our relationship.

"Once upon a time I was a boy from the wrong side of town. Now I'm Ryder Hayes, just a man. I can't go back. And loving you, a girl who was too fine for that boy from The Creek, was as much a part of my identity back then as being Billy Hayes's son. With you that past, my past, is too close."

She worked to even her breathing. "What are you saying?"

"This isn't going to work, Jennifer."

"Don't do this," she whispered, panic threading through her words. "We've been through so much . . . we've waited so long for each other. I was wrong just now, I was wrong back then. I'm sorry. We can put this behind us and go on. Give me another chance, Ryder . . . give us another chance. I love you."

Ryder drew away, her words jackknifing through him. He would have given everything he had to hear those words just days ago, but now to hear them when it was too late was agony.

He surrendered to the urge and touched her hair for the last time. The strands were unbelievably soft against his fingertips, and he wondered if that sensation, like everything else about her, would live on in his memory forever, surfacing to taunt him at the exact moment he'd thought he'd gotten over her.

"I know who I am and what I am," he said, his tone rough. "I need someone who believes in me—wholeheartedly. I deserve that, Jen. I've earned it. And with you there'll always be doubt."

He dropped his hand. "I'd always wonder if someday something would happen and everything I thought we had would be reduced to nothing again."

The sound she made came from someplace deep inside her. She felt as if her heart were being torn from her, the light extinguished from her life.

Jennifer stiffened against the pain. She couldn't have lost him, it couldn't be over. "You love me, I know you do." Fighting tears, she inched her chin up. "How can you throw that away?"

"Not me, Jen. You're the one who threw it away."

Jennifer shook her head against the tears that wanted to spill over, against the finality of his words. "You're not being fair," she said brokenly. "You talk about the importance of belief, of trust, yet you outright told me you couldn't believe in me. You confessed your love, then told me you couldn't 'escape' it. So if I didn't wholeheartedly believe in you, neither did you in me."

"But I never betrayed you."

She wasn't going to cry, not again. "Didn't you?" she asked, meeting his eyes. "I made a lot of mistakes, but I refuse to think I'm the one who did everything wrong. And I refuse to be the bad guy."

"Funny, I've been the bad guy for years."

Feeling as if he'd slapped her, she took a step back. "You're right. We'll never be just Jennifer and Ryder...not if you won't let us." She hiked her purse up on her shoulder. "It looks to me like I'm not the only one who needs to face the past."

Without another word she turned and walked away.

Chapter Twelve

Jennifer stared up at Sonny's old house, her fingers curled in a death grip around the steering wheel. The days had slipped by, one into another, just as the seconds and minutes and hours had. Time had passed without a ripple, as if a week ago her heart hadn't been shattered into a billion pieces.

She'd run into Ryder several times—at the dry cleaners, outside the Short Stack—had seen him running on The Green. And each time had been painful beyond comprehension.

The times they'd come face-to-face, his eyes had been cool, his tone distant when he'd greeted her. It was as if there'd never been anything between them, let alone a fire that had burned so brightly as to be blinding.

So she'd come here, to Sonny's, to this symbol of her eighteenth year. Because all her answers lay in her past. She hadn't fully understood that when she'd flung those final words at Ryder; she did now.

For long moments, Jennifer gazed at the house. Sucking in a sharp breath, she grabbed her purse, stepped from the car and strode determinedly up the walk. For the first time in forever, she knew exactly what she was doing and why.

She let herself into the large, familiar home, not giving herself time to reconsider, not pausing until she had the door closed behind her.

Inside, she did as she and Ryder had done weeks before. Only this time, as she went from room to room, she didn't let her emotions overwhelm her—she remembered not as a hurting eighteen-year-old girl, but as a woman determined to face her fears and go on.

She ended up in the living room and sank onto the thick carpeting.

Sonny. He'd been beautiful and golden, the quintessential all-American boy. She smiled, remembering the way he had strutted, the way he'd hugged and kissed them all, the way he'd cajoled.

He'd been a consummate actor. He'd known how to use his smile to charm, to melt a girl's heart in order to get what he wanted. His mother used to laugh that he'd developed that ability in the cradle.

Jennifer plucked at the thick pile, her smile fading. He had played the three of them—her and Cyndi and Meredith—against each other. Ryder had said that to her the night of the prom, but she'd been unable—or unwilling—to see the truth of his words back then. She saw it now.

How many times had Sonny pulled her aside to confide to her his dissatisfaction with Cyndi? Or to murmur how he wished Cyndi liked sports or was as daring as she? How many times had he lingered over his kiss to her cheek, or held her hand a moment too long for friends?

A lot. Jennifer shook her head. And each time he'd done so, he'd increased the competition between the already competitive girls, increased the wedge of distance between them. After all, how could she have confided Sonny's actions or her own feelings to either of her friends?

She couldn't have. So she'd kept secrets. And her guilt had grown.

She wasn't to blame for Sonny's death. Jennifer expelled a long breath, a breath that seemed to come from a place so deep inside her she wondered if she'd been holding it for a decade.

The night of the prom Sonny had tried to manipulate her, just as he'd manipulated her so many times before. But her head had been filled with Ryder, with the truth of what he'd said to her in the garden and with the way he made her feel. So that night, for the first time, she'd turned Sonny away.

In those moments she'd seen the real Sonny, had seen his selfishness and how little he really cared about her feelings.

Even as anger ran through her, Jennifer shook it off. Just as Sonny hadn't been the perfect hero she'd painted him to be, he hadn't been evil, either. He'd been an adolescent boy, testing his power, his prowess. He'd been selfish and thoroughly spoiled. And he had enjoyed basking in the attention of the three most popular girls at school.

Because Meredith had been besotted, as well. Jennifer rolled her eyes, remembering the times she'd seen Sonny and Meredith whispering together or lingering at lockers in the morning, remembering the glances, the smiles, the awkward silences. She'd been a naive fool not to have seen the truth back then. No wonder Ryder had laughed at them all.

Ryder.

Where Sonny had been golden and charming, Ryder had been dark and intense. And instead of toying with the world as Sonny had, he'd faced it. Angrily at times, but always squarely. He hadn't played games, and he'd always been there for her. He'd been the only one.

Jennifer drew in a deep shuddering breath and covered her face with her hands. Dear God, it was Ryder she'd loved all along.

Her breath caught at the truth of that, lodging painfully in her throat. She'd loved Ryder but she hadn't believed in him. She'd professed to love Sonny, but what she'd loved had been an image, the fairy-tale hero she'd fabricated, not a flesh-and-blood person.

Her tears spilled over. She'd loved Ryder then. She loved him now. Not with the love she'd thought she'd had a few weeks ago—but deeply, passionately and without reservation.

Ryder was the only man she'd ever loved. And now she'd lost him.

Pain a living thing inside her, Jennifer wrapped her arms around her chest. She cried for what was and what could have been, her sobs echoing in the empty house.

Ryder pressed the heels of his hands to his eyes and muttered several short, severe words. The week since he and Jennifer had parted had been awful. He hadn't thought it could get any worse, hadn't thought he could become any more disillusioned.

His lips twisted. It seemed he'd been a naive fool to believe that.

Ryder looked up at Jennifer's parents' home. It hadn't changed much. The trees and bushes had filled out, but the house itself was still painted white with dark green shutters, the lawn was as well trimmed, the gardens as lush as they had been ten years ago.

Ryder sucked in a deep breath and swung off the bike. After unstrapping his briefcase, he moved slowly up the walk, remembering the hundreds of times he had done the same.

He stopped at the front door. He doubted there would be any kind of welcome for him today, just as there had never been for him in the past.

Henry Joyce answered on the first knock. Ryder saw he'd been right about what to expect.

"Hayes."

"Joyce." Ryder tapped the envelope-style case against his leg. "Can I come in?"

The other man stared at him, his eyes narrowed, his square jaw tight with either anger, dislike or more likely, a combination of the two. After a moment, he stepped aside.

Ryder looked around the familiar foyer, noting again that not much had changed. He shifted his gaze to the staircase and for a moment was eighteen again and watching the girl of his dreams descend in a cloud of peach.

Jennifer.

Pain shot through him, and he jerked his gaze back to the older man. "I have something to discuss with you, something I think you might be interested in."

"I wouldn't count on it."

Without comment, Ryder handed him the correspondence he'd received from Lansing's headquarters that morning.

Henry read it over, then looked back up at him. "What is this?"

"I think that's obvious. We're being jacked around by the corporation."

"We?" He handed the paper back. "I'm not an employee of Lansing anymore, remember?"

"But you're a citizen of Hazelhurst. You care what happens to this town."

Henry nodded, acceding the point but not budging from his position just inside the doorway.

"Is there somewhere we can sit down?"

Henry paused a moment, then led him to the kitchen. When they'd settled across from each other at the table, Ryder took a file folder from his briefcase and slid it across to the other man. "This file contains my original proposal to Lansing. The corporation guaranteed that if I could convince the men, and the union, to agree to a dollar-an-hour wage reduction with a promise of no contract renegotiations for three years, they would keep the plant open. I did that.''

Henry scanned through the documents. ''Damn good proposal,'' he muttered, his tone grudging.

Ryder slid the morning's correspondence across the table. ''Again, this is what I received today. A dollar an hour isn't enough anymore. They want two.''

''The men will never agree.''

''I'd never even ask.'' Ryder fixed Henry with a level stare. ''It's obvious to me now what's going on.... Lansing wants to shut us down unless the profit margin is so great as to be ridiculous. Maybe I'm wrong, but I think it's been their plan all along. They sent me in, probably knowing some of my past history with Hazelhurst, anticipating a jaundiced perspective on my part. The last thing they expected me to do was pull a rabbit out of the hat. Nor, when they offered, did they anticipate the men agreeing to that wage cut.''

''Why the fanfare? Why not just do it?''

Ryder made a sound of frustration and leaned back in his chair. ''I'm not certain, but I have a few ideas. They're a public corporation, they may be worried about adverse press. A lot of small, one-industry towns have fallen because increased foreign competition has forced American plants to shut down.''

''And Lansing's just opened a couple of foreign plants—''

''Who make similar products,'' Ryder finished for him. ''Also, if you remember, last year their chemical division was involved in a huge environmental scandal, and the year before that there were a couple of nasty discrimination suits brought against them."

Henry drummed his fingers on the kitchen table-top. "Or could there be some sort of corporate game-playing going on here?"

"That's my other guess. Mississippi has done some pretty hard campaigning for industry and supposedly it was us or a sister plant there." Ryder shrugged. "I've seen that plant's figures and frankly, it was a toss-up without the wage cut."

"Somebody high up could have already made up their mind. Or," Henry muttered, "had their palms greased. We may never know for sure."

"We'll *probably* never know."

"Those bastards."

"Tell me about it."

The older man was silent for a moment, then met his eyes. "So, why are you here, Hayes? Just to fill me in?"

Ryder rested his elbows on the table and leaned forward. "I have a proposition for you."

Henry arched his brows. "For me? I thought I'd been terminated."

"Not on my order. I suspect you know that already, but if not—" he nudged the file containing his proposal toward the other man "—it's right in front of you in black and white."

"You recommended I stay because of Jennifer," the other man said bitterly.

Ryder worked to keep his reaction to her name from showing. But the now-familiar pain curled through him, making the past minutes—minutes free from thoughts of her—seem like the most carefree of his life.

He concentrated on the other man, using their immediate problem as an anesthetic. "No, not because of...Jennifer. I find many of your management techniques faulty—"

"Ditto."

"Especially," Ryder continued, affected not at all by the other man's venom, "when it comes to dealing with the workers." He met Henry's gaze. "But you know how to keep a plant running. Day in and day out, smooth as silk."

"So?"

The older man bit the question off, but still Ryder could tell he'd been pleased by the comment. "So, that's why I'm here. Interested enough to listen to the rest?"

Henry folded his arms across his chest and rocked back in his chair. "I've got lots of time these days."

"Okay then, here's the deal. Lansing wants to close us down. Close the plant and Hazelhurst's had it. It's the same situation that's been cropping up all over the country. I propose the same solution many others have."

Henry snapped forward, the front legs of the chair hitting the floor with a thud. "An employee buy-out. We use the plant's assets as leverage to secure the loan."

"Bingo."

"You think the workers will go for it?"

"Others all over the country have. Besides, let's look at the alternatives . . . no job here, no way to sell a home and leave, damn few jobs in manufacturing even if they do pack up. And those are the negatives. On the positive side, they'll be getting a piece of the pie. They'll have a real say in policies and working conditions. And it's an investment. Times get better, so does the money."

"Hmm . . ." Henry rocked back in his chair once more, thoughtfully rubbing his chin. "It could work."

"You bet it could." Ryder sent another folder across to Henry. "I've done some preliminary figuring."

Henry read it over, nodding his head now and then, murmuring his agreement. He met Ryder's eyes once more. "Are these figures pretty accurate?"

"They're negotiable."

Henry closed the file. "Okay, Hayes. What's my part in this?"

Ryder smiled. "Every ship needs a captain, every team a leader. You're that man."

"Considering our history, I'm not sure I heard you correctly."

"You heard correctly."

"What about you? You don't fancy heading up this deal?"

"I'm not a leader." Ryder paused a moment, waiting for Henry to agree. The older man didn't, though an hour ago he would have, and Ryder smiled a little. "The men like me, true. They know they can tell me the bald truth without fear of repercussions. They know I'll go to bat for them. But I'm too much one of them to be their leader."

Ryder folded his hands on the table in front of him. "On the other hand, the men don't like you. But they respect you. You've kept this boat afloat for a lot of years, and there are a number of men still around who remember the old days before you came in. They'll rally around you, and they'll trust you in that lead spot...trust you to keep the plant running for them."

Ryder could see the other man warming to the idea and grinned. "But I warn you, as part owners, they're going to be more demanding about what they want and more vocal. I wouldn't be surprised if they request some of those 'bleeding heart' programs you despise."

Henry laughed, loudly and with gusto. "Will you be staying on?"

Jennifer. She filled his head, his heart. It suddenly seemed as if there weren't enough air in the room. He couldn't imagine what it would be like to live in the same town with her, day in and day out, and not be able to be with her.

"No," Ryder managed, feeling real regret at having to leave Hazelhurst. He'd grown more fond of it then he ever could have imagined, more fond than was wise.

Henry was silent for several moments, then cleared his throat. "What about my daughter?"

Ryder met the other man's eyes. "I don't see where that relates to the issue at hand."

"We're talking about decisions that would affect her life, too, if she's going to be a part of yours. I think I'm within my rights to ask."

"Then I think you should ask your daughter."

"I'm asking you."

Ryder drew a deep breath and faced the other man squarely. "Jennifer won't be coming with me."

"I see."

Did he? Ryder wondered, watching as the other man picked the proposal up once more. Did he see what a great part he had played in that answer? Did he understand how much it hurt Ryder not to be able to proudly claim her?

After a moment, Henry cleared his throat again and set the proposal aside. "If you change your mind...about leaving...well, I think we might make a pretty good team."

In other words, if he changed his mind about Jennifer, it would be okay, he wouldn't stand in their way. Ryder leaned back in his chair, stunned, feeling as if he were being torn in two.

Then he slowly shook his head. "I won't be."

The other man drummed his fingers on the tabletop for a moment. "If that's your decision—"

"It is."

"What's next then?"

"A powwow with the employees. I was thinking about Saturday morning."

Henry inclined his head. "Let's do it."

Her parents' house was bathed in twilight. Jennifer pulled into the driveway, then climbed out of the car. She didn't have to look into a mirror to know that her face had been ravaged by her tears, she knew it by the ache in every muscle of her body and the throbbing at her temples.

She wished she could be as certain of why she was here.

She started toward the front door, stopping when she noticed Ryder's bike. She looked from it to the door, her pulse beginning to throb.

What was Ryder doing here?

Just then he stepped out of the house, turning to say goodbye to her parents. Jennifer stood rooted to the spot, halfway between the front door and her car, torn between running toward him and away.

When he turned back around, his eyes met hers. Without smiling, he closed the distance between them. "Hello, Jen."

"Ryder," she said softly, her mouth dry, her heart beating almost out of control.

"How have you been?" he asked.

"Fine." She caught her bottom lip between her teeth, searching desperately for the right thing to say, cursing the cool, guarded look in his eyes.

"Great." He looked around. "Pretty sunset."

A hysterical laugh bubbled to her lips. They, who had reached into each other's souls, were resorting to talking about the weather. She slipped her shaking hands into her pockets and wished something so simple could take care of her heart, as well.

"Yes," she said, shifting her gaze to the fiery sunset. The colors were already fading, slipping beyond the horizon. Soon they would both be bathed in darkness. She looked back at him, and for a moment she thought she saw something warm and aching in his eyes. Something that reached out to her. Then it was gone.

"Goodbye, Jen."

He turned and walked away. She let him. For a long time she just stood there, too numbed by despair to move. Then, when the darkness had crept over her, she turned and moved slowly toward her parents' front door.

She let herself in, not calling out. Her parents were in the dining room, readying for supper.

And the moment she saw them, Jennifer knew exactly why she had come.

"Mom, Dad, I need to talk to you."

Her parents looked up at her, shocked at her appearance. "Jennifer...my God, what's happened—"

"Nothing. I just needed to talk to you."

"Sit down, honey." Her father patted the seat next to his. "Your mother and I have some things to discuss with you as well."

Jennifer shook her head. "No. What I have to say has to come first, and I prefer to stand while I do."

Seeing their astonished expressions, she plowed on before they could comment. "You're my parents, my family, and I love you. I care what you think, and I hate disappointing you. I always have. But I have to do what's right for me."

She took another deep breath. "And Ryder's right for me. I'm in love with him."

When her parents only stared blankly at her, Jennifer inched her chin up and narrowed her eyes. "I've loved him since high school. I believe in him. I trust him and his judgment."

She shifted her gaze to her father's. "He didn't recommend your termination, Dad. I don't care what it *looks* like. He fought to save the plant and your job, and he deserves to be thanked not vilified.''

''We didn't realize—'' Henry cleared his throat ''—we didn't know you felt...this strongly about him.''

''I should have told you a long time ago. I treated Ryder badly, twice now, and I wouldn't blame him if he didn't give me another chance. But if he will, I'm going to take it. No matter what either of you think.''

''Honey, we—''

Jennifer sent her mother a warning glance. ''And another thing—his name is Ryder. I never want to hear you call him 'that boy' again. Ever. Got that?''

Her mother's eyes widened and she sat back in her chair. ''Yes, honey.''

''Are you finished?'' her father asked quietly.

Jennifer nodded, swallowing hard.

''Then I suggest you sit down.''

She did as he asked and a moment later was glad she had.

''What did you say?''

''That Ryder and I are working together on a leveraged buy-out of the plant.''

Jennifer looked at her mother for confirmation, and the other woman nodded. ''When...did this happen?''

''Just today.'' Her father sketched in the details for her, adding when he'd finished, ''I know Ryder wasn't responsible for Lansing's actions. I suspected all along. But I wanted to believe he was because it was a whole lot easier on my pride.''

He folded his hands in his lap. ''Try to understand, Jennifer, I was angry—at him, at the world. That job, that plant, meant everything to me." Her father lowered his voice. "I'm sorry if I've ruined things for you. The things I said and did were wrong."

Jennifer stood and crossed to him, kneeling down by his chair. "No, Dad, you didn't ruin it. I did. It's nobody's fault but my own."

She laid her head on his knees, he stroked her hair and asked. "Is there anything I can do?"

She shook her head. "I've made the mess, I've got to clean it up." She met his eyes. "That's part of being an adult."

He looked at her wistfully. "You really are all grown-up, baby girl."

She smiled at the contradiction. "I love you, Dad."

Chapter Thirteen

Jennifer sat at the back of the overflowing auditorium, heart in her throat and fingers crossed as she watched her father up on the stage. He appeared every inch the vibrant, confident leader she remembered from her childhood, only now she understood he wasn't an infallible hero—he was just a man.

Jennifer looked from the man she'd loved as a girl to the man she loved as a woman, the man she had wronged and now didn't know if she could live without.

Tears welled in her eyes, and she blinked against them. How was she going to face the next day and the next, how could she smile at the future when she knew he would never be a part of it?

She dragged her gaze back to her father as he began to speak. You could have heard a pin drop in the crowded auditorium as he explained the situation and Lansing's request for further wage cuts. If possible, the room became quieter still as he presented his and Ryder's proposal for an employee buy-out.

The moment of almost electric silence passed as with a shout, the entire auditorium got to its feet. Jennifer let her pent-up breath out in a rush. The employees had not only gone for it, they had done so wholeheartedly.

On the stage her father and Ryder slapped each other on the back in congratulations. Around her, pandemonium had broken out.

In a moment, she knew, her father would step back and let Ryder take the podium. Ryder would explain the nuts and bolts of the buy-out and give them the bottom line.

She couldn't stay and watch him. It would hurt too much, it already did. Jennifer stood and inched her way to the aisle, then slipped out of the auditorium to the sound of Ryder calling order back to the room.

The sound of his voice was like a knife twisting inside her, just as watching the camaraderie between him and her father had been. The irony of it was almost too much to bear. The thing she'd always dreamed of had happened—a split second after she had tossed it all away.

Jennifer stepped out of the town hall and into the brilliant sunshine. She found it ironic also that Ryder and her father should have chosen the morning of her class reunion for the plant employees to vote Hazelhurst's fate.

She hurried to her car, focusing on the things she still needed to take care of before evening arrived, trying hard not to think of Ryder or the meeting she would have with her two old friends that night.

Jennifer took the way she always did, by the small, hilly cemetery where Sonny was buried. And as she had every time since that rainy morning ten years ago, she looked toward his grave and the elaborate marker his parents had placed there for him.

Today he wasn't alone.

There were two women standing alongside his grave, two women Jennifer recognized even though a decade had passed since she'd seen them last.

A trembling started in the pit of her stomach and spread. She pulled the car to a stop and drew in a deep, steadying breath. She didn't think she was up to this, didn't think she was ready to face them. She could keep driving, meet them tonight instead—when she'd had time to prepare herself, time to plan what she would say.

She reached for the gearshift to put the car back into drive, then dropped her hand.

Real friends didn't have to prepare to see each other.

Jennifer clutched the steering wheel with shaking fingers and looked back toward the women. Cyndi's hair was as gloriously blond as it had ever been, shimmering in the sun, being lifted slightly by the breeze.

Jennifer closed her eyes, reminded of a snatch of her—their—past that she hadn't thought of in years.

It had been the first day of their senior year. They'd all been out in the parking lot, waiting for the morning bell, leaning on and admiring Sonny's sporty new car.

"Back to school," Sonny had muttered. "Bummer."

She had turned to him, laughing. "How can you say that, Sonny Keighton? This is our senior year! We've waited three years for our turn to be number one. It's going to be great!"

"And you're going to take the team to another championship," Cyndi said softly, cuddling a little closer to his side. "I can't wait to see your first touchdown. I'm going to cheer my lungs out for you."

Ryder, leaning indolently against the car, his face lifted to the sun, cast the other boy an amused glance. "Yeah, Sonny-boy. Another chance to show us all how wonderful you are."

"Hey, buddy—" Sonny flipped Ryder the bird and the girls laughed.

"Next year college," Meredith said suddenly, in the way she always did—out of the blue.

"And the future," Cyndi added dreamily, looking up at Sonny.

Jennifer placed her fists on her hips and tossed back her head. "I can't believe you two! We're only beginning our senior year and you guys have already moved on. I guess I'll have to have enough fun for all of us." She turned to Ryder. "What about you, Ryder? What do you think?"

He looked at her then, a corner of his mouth lifting in the small smirk that tied her stomach into knots. "It's cool. There are a lot worse places to hang."

The bell sounded and Ryder pushed away from the car. "Time to head in."

"Like cattle," Sonny muttered again, sliding off the hood.

"But really," Meredith said as they started for the building. "What do you think we'll all be doing ten years from now?"

Jennifer shuddered and once more looked over at her old friends. Could any of them have imagined this on that innocent autumn day?

Taking a deep breath, she opened the car door and stepped out.

Although not yet fall, it was already in the air—a coolness, a clarity that was lost during the worst heat of the summer. The leaves were still green, the grass lush, but the smells had changed from potent to subtle, the colors from vibrant to hushed.

It was the same with her friends. Cyndi was still the perfect blond-haired beauty; Meredith's beauty was still of the quiet, flawless variety. Yet both had changed, their looks seeming enhanced, deepened, with age.

Jennifer looked down at herself, comparing Cyndi's sundress and Meredith's crisp cotton slacks and blouse to her own jeans and T-shirt. What would they think of the way she'd changed? Would they wonder, as she did, how three such different women could have become such a big part of one another's lives back then?

Cyndi saw her first and turned and smiled. "Jennifer."

Meredith turned in greeting, also. Hers was the same smile Jennifer remembered from all those years ago, but somehow warmer, less remote.

"Hi," Jennifer murmured, the word sounding forced even to her own ears. She cleared her throat. "When did you guys get into town?"

"Last night," Cyndi said.

"And we drove in early this morning."

"We?" Jennifer asked, her eyes going to Meredith's left hand. A plain gold band circled her fourth finger.

"My husband Garrett and I." Meredith's expression softened, and she placed a hand protectively over her abdomen. "We were married in June."

Cyndi turned to Meredith, her eyes wide. "You're kidding. Nick and I were married last month!"

Jennifer thought of Ryder, and the ache that never went away these days, deepened. She shifted her gaze to the horizon. Neither of the women had asked if she was married, no doubt they already knew she was not. Silence fell between them once more.

Cyndi broke it first. "I'm really glad to be back." She shook her head and laughed, the sound light but cautious. "I never thought I'd say that."

"I know what you mean," Meredith agreed, smiling.

"Well, I never left," Jennifer said. Hurt was there in her voice, hurt and a bit of accusation. She couldn't have held it back even if she'd wanted to.

Honesty, she told herself and met her old friends' gazes once more. "Why, after all this time, after not one word, have you come back? Not for the reunion."

"No," Meredith said quietly, meeting her eyes, "not for the reunion." She lowered her eyes for a moment, then lifted them back to Jennifer's. "I was back once before, Jen. I thought of you...I wondered how you were doing and how life had treated you—" her voice faltered "—but I wasn't ready to be here. It was a bad time for me and...I couldn't have faced you. I still felt too guilty."

She paused, placing a hand on her abdomen once again. "I still blamed myself for Sonny's death."

Jennifer made some sound, of denial, of surprise. She shifted her gaze to Cyndi and saw the other woman's expression was also one of shock.

"But I blamed myself," Jennifer said.

"And I did, too," Cyndi whispered, obviously shaken.

The three looked at each other. Jennifer cleared her throat. "At the after-prom party, Sonny cornered me in the equipment room. He was acting strangely, like he'd been all night. He told me he needed me...and that he had to talk to me. But I was upset, too. Ryder and I had had a fight and my head was filled with...the things we'd said to each other. I told Sonny to go find you, Cyndi. That was the last time I saw him."

Jennifer shook her head, thinking of the parts she'd left out of the story and of the things she'd learned since. "I felt so guilty...like such a—" She drew a deep breath. "I felt I should have seen how much Sonny needed me, how out of control he was. For years I punished myself for not being a better friend to him. I kept thinking if I'd taken the time to talk to him he wouldn't have gotten on the bike and—''

''Oh, Jennifer,'' Cyndi cut in. ''I feel terrible that all those years you blamed yourself. If only we'd talked, you would have known the true story.''

Cyndi looked down at her hands, to the diamond solitaire and gold band that graced her left hand. She touched it, a soft smile curving her lips. The unconscious simplicity of the gesture twisted in Jennifer's gut. It implied trust and devotion, lives shared and happily ever after. All the things she would never have with Ryder.

''Those last months of high school,'' Cyndi said finally, softly, looking back up at her two friends, ''those months before the prom were so... difficult. I was desperately in love with Sonny, and I was losing him. I knew that, I'd even admitted it to myself.''

She shifted her gaze to the distance, her cheeks tinting ever so slightly with the same rose of her sundress. ''He'd been pressuring me for months to...make love. But I couldn't. That good girls didn't had been ingrained so deeply in me and, who knows, maybe in my heart of hearts I knew it wasn't right. But whatever the reason, I wasn't ready.

''But I'd decided if saying yes to Sonny was the only way I was going to be able to hold on to him, that's what I would do. Prom night was going to be 'the' night.''

Jennifer's heart went out to her friend, and her eyes filled with tears. She moved her gaze to Meredith's and saw that her eyes, too, were full.

"From the moment he picked me up, that night was a disaster." Cyndi laced her fingers together. "I thought he was treating me so badly because I was a disappointment to him, and I still hoped saying yes would make everything all right again."

She sighed heavily and Jennifer knew how difficult this was for her. "I offered myself to him, then at the last moment, I couldn't go through with it. Sonny said terrible things to me, horrible things. He looked me in the eyes and told me everything was my fault, and that if I'd been a real woman he wouldn't be in the mess he was in now."

Meredith gasped and brought a hand to her mouth, her cheeks draining of color. Cyndi looked at her for a moment then went on. "We broke up that night. And like both of you, the next morning I learned he was dead. I blamed myself. I believed those things he said to me, the things he called me. I know now he was just young and confused, and that I'm not to blame for his death."

She turned to her old friends. "But I never have been able to understand what was going on that night. With all of us. It was so weird, so Kafkaesque."

"There was no way you could have, Cyndi," Meredith said softly, the tiniest tremor in her voice. "No way either of you could."

She caught her lower lip between her teeth and tipped her face up to the sky. When she looked back at them, her eyes were glassy and her lips trembled. "I was pregnant, you guys. The baby was . . . Sonny's."

The gasp came from Cyndi; Jennifer was certain she couldn't have made a sound. Even the breeze seemed to pause, the birds to quiet.

A tear spilled over and ran down Meredith's cheek. She met Cyndi's eyes. "I'm sorry, Cyndi. I never meant to hurt you."

The three girls looked at each other, none knowing quite what to say.

In that moment Jennifer knew, maybe for the first time, what it was to be an adult. Hands shaking, she clasped them together in front of her. "I thought I was in love with Sonny, too," she murmured, adding a piece to her story that she'd left out earlier. "Nothing ever happened, but he knew and he encouraged me. Manipulated my feelings." She looked at Cyndi. "I felt so guilty about my secret love for your boyfriend."

Cyndi touched her wedding set again, then smiled softly at her two friends, telling them without words that it was okay. "What happened, Meredith?"

"I told him at the prom...when we danced. We had a terrible fight. It was awful...he said some things that...he even suggested I have..."

She didn't finish the thought, obviously finding it too painful. "Until then I thought he loved me—" heat stained her cheeks "—and I thought I loved him."

She paused to pull herself to together. "Long before today I'd come to terms with who Sonny was and the reality of what it was that we shared. But for a long time I blamed myself for his death. If I hadn't sprung the news on him then, if I'd waited..."

Meredith shook her head. "No high school senior is emotionally capable of handling that kind of a bomb. We were both upset and made mistakes. We both did the best we could with the resources we had."

"What happened to..." Jennifer let her words trail off.

"The baby?"

Jennifer nodded.

Meredith swallowed, her eyes filling once more. "I gave her up. For years I was angry about it. I blamed everyone for that decision but myself." She shifted her gaze to Sonny's grave. "This last year I had to face the fact that *I'd* given my baby up and that I couldn't redo the past or go on punishing myself for it."

She turned back to her old friends, the tears brimming over, spilling down her cheeks. "I made the right decision for me...but most of all, for our baby. I saw her, you guys... she's so beautiful, so well loved and happy."

"Oh, Meredith..." Jennifer put her arms around her, then Cyndi around them both. "I wish I could have been there for you. I wish I could have helped you through that."

"Me, too," Cyndi whispered, her voice choked with tears.

"I needed you guys so badly." Meredith tightened her arms. "I wish I'd had the guts to tell you, to ask you for help. Especially when I see how my decision has affected you both."

She shook her head, hiccuping. "I always thought you two had just gone on." She looked first at Cyndi, then Jennifer. "You deserved better than I gave you, and I'm sorry I didn't say goodbye.'' She swiped at the tears on her cheeks. ''You both meant a lot to me.''

''I regret we weren't closer,'' Cyndi said as they drew apart. ''I regret I wasn't a better friend to the both of you.'' She dug in her purse for a handkerchief. ''I was so frightened back then...so frightened that I'd do or say something inappropriate and suddenly I wouldn't be the perfect little princess anymore. I was so busy pretending and keeping up appearances that I didn't allow myself to feel.''

Jennifer wiped her eyes, her hands trembling almost out of control. ''I always thought of you as the one who had everything.''

''It was all a costly illusion. I was a confused little girl with no one to talk to about that confusion.''

''You had us,'' Meredith said quietly, the expression in her eyes bittersweet. ''You just didn't know it. None of us knew what we had.''

''I was the only one of us who thought we were really friends,'' Jennifer said. ''And in the time since, I've always hurt when I thought of you both, hurt and felt betrayed.''

Cyndi reached out. ''Oh, Jennifer, I'm so—''

Jennifer squeezed the other woman's outstretched hand but shook her head. ''I realized recently that I'd held back from you both as well. I never told you how I really felt—feelings were too personal, too close. I wasn't the friend I wanted to be, not to you two...and not to Ryder.''

''Ryder?'' both women repeated, surprised.

''He's back, too, after ten years.'' Jennifer looked each women in the eye as if daring them to say a word against him. "I'm in love with him. I always have been."

Her eyes brimmed with tears, but she didn't try to hide them. "I've hurt him. Because I couldn't face my past, couldn't see it and my feelings for Sonny for what they were." She angled her chin up. "But I see now, and I'm going to find a way, somehow, to show him I do believe in him, that we deserve another chance."

As the words passed her lips, Jennifer realized they were true. She wouldn't give up, they'd been through too much for that. She would fight for him. She would beg if she had to, would, if necessary, spend the next ten years proving she was deserving of his love and trust and showing him that what they felt for each other was worth putting their hearts on the line for.

"You know," Meredith said sadly, "the tragedy of this is, if we had talked to each other, if we had gone to each other for support, none of this would have happened."

She smiled at her friends. "Today I came to tell Sonny about his daughter. I've done that now... it's time to go."

Cyndi plucked a wildflower from the lush grass at her feet. "I wanted to say goodbye to Sonny as an adult. I felt I needed to touch this part of my past to finally lay it to rest." She laid the flower on the grave and stepped back.

Silence fell between them, but not the awkward silence of earlier. Peaceful, Jennifer thought. Peaceful and healing.

"It's all about growing up, isn't it?" she remarked then, thinking of herself and Ryder, of the future they would build and of how far they'd come together.

"And friendship," Cyndi added.

"Sonny's girls." Jennifer laughed. "That's what Ryder always called us."

"We haven't been those for a long time." Meredith smiled. "We're three women...three *friends* who share an awful lot of past."

Jennifer wasn't sure who moved first, but suddenly they had their arms wrapped around one another and were crying and laughing and being the kind of friends they'd always wanted to be but had never quite known how to.

Now they knew. And today they were touching the future instead of the past.

After a while they broke apart, sniffling, giggling, wiping tears from their cheeks. Meredith turned to Jennifer, a smile curving her mouth. "Does the Short Stack still make those incredible chocolate sodas?"

"They sure do."

Cyndi gasped. "I can't, I shouldn't . . . the camera adds pounds and magnifies..." Helplessly she gave in. "Do they still have the strawberry sundaes, too?"

Laughing, the three women walked arm in arm down the grassy hill, away from Sonny's grave for the last time.

Chapter Fourteen

The reunion was held at the Hazelhurst Country Club, just as the prom had been. Jennifer stood in front of the ornate gold-leaf mirror in the ladies' lounge, absently checking her reflection, using the moments to clear her head.

It was unsettling seeing all her old classmates again—it had been so long, they'd all changed so much. But in a strange way everyone was just as they'd been all those years ago.

Jennifer smiled, thinking of Cyndi and Meredith. It had been wonderful being with her old friends again. That afternoon they'd gone to the Short Stack and indulged in the overrich ice creams. They'd talked and laughed and caught up. Meredith had told them about the scholarship she'd been awarded and of her plans to go on until she had her doctorate. Then, when

Meredith had told them she was pregnant, she and Cyndi had squealed and pushed their remaining desserts her way.

Cyndi had talked of her cable show, of how terrified she'd first been and how Nick had challenged her until she'd had to find the strength she'd never known she had.

And then, finally, Jennifer's turn had come, and she'd shared Ryder with them, their story from the past and the present. She'd told them about the happenings at the Hazelhurst plant, and had learned that blaming Ryder for Sonny's death had never even crossed either of their minds.

Jennifer pushed at the wisps of hair that fell over her forehead. Their encouragement and support of her feelings had felt better than anything had in a long time, and for the rest of the day she'd been imbued with optimism.

But with the evening, with the reliving of the past and talk of the future, her optimism had waned, leaving in its place an aching loneliness—an ache only Ryder could ease.

"Hey, are you okay?"

Jennifer looked up as Cyndi stepped into the lounge. She smiled weakly. "Fine."

Cyndi sank onto the striped satin settee and took a lipstick from her evening bag. "Meredith and Craig Smythe are catching up. Garrett's watching them like a hawk." She applied the rose hue, then dropped the tube back into her evening bag. "He's gorgeous, don't you think?"

"Yes." Jennifer smiled. "Although he looks more like a stevedore than a professor of English literature."

"What do you think of Nick?"

The question took Jennifer aback—the Cyndi of old would never have been so forthright—but only for a moment. "Besides fabulously handsome?" she asked. When her friend nodded, Jennifer cocked her head in thought. "Strong. Dependable. Somehow fierce. Especially when it comes to you. I like him."

Cyndi's expression softened. "I do, too."

A lump formed in her throat, and Jennifer turned back to the mirror, rummaging in her own bag for a lipstick.

"You're missing Ryder."

Helplessly Jennifer met her friend's eyes in the mirror. "Does it show that much?"

"Yes."

Jennifer sighed and gave up all pretense of looking for the lipstick. "I'd hoped he'd come. I'm not surprised he didn't, but I had hoped."

She turned away from the mirror. "I feel so odd—like I'm experiencing the world from behind a gray screen. Only when I'm with Ryder do I get the full-color picture. I keep wanting to turn and share a thought or observation with him. I'm a grown woman who can take care of herself, yet without his support I feel a little lost, a little out of step."

"Boy, do I recognize those symptoms." Cyndi crossed her legs and smoothed the skirt of her simple black sheath. "Have you figured out your next move?"

"As soon as I'm able, I'm going to slip away from here and see if I can find him. The question is, what am I going to do once I have him cornered."

"Is everything all right in here?" Meredith poked her head around the door.

"Come on in. Jennifer's thinking up a plan."

Meredith laughed and stepped into the room. "Where have I heard that before?" When neither of the other girls laughed, she sobered. "This is about Ryder."

Jennifer perched miserably on the edge of the counter. "Any ideas?"

"Hmm." Meredith tapped her index finger against her mouth. "Well, if learning from experience has taught me anything, I'd try the direct, honest approach."

Cyndi nodded. "Sage advice, Jen."

"I agree." Jennifer frowned. "But how do I get him to listen? The last time I saw him he wouldn't even look at me, let alone stand and listen."

"He'll listen," Meredith said slowly. "From everything you've told us he's as wildly in love with you as you are with him. He won't be able not to."

"I agree," Cyndi said, standing and putting her arm around Jennifer's shoulder. "And if that doesn't work, try handcuffs."

Meredith grinned. "Or a lasso."

"Or kidnapping."

"Or—"

Jennifer shook her head, laughing despite the butterflies in her stomach. "It's not that I don't appreciate the help, guys..."

They made their way back to the ballroom, stopping in surprise as Cyndi's name was called from the stage.

"The awards," Jennifer whispered, elbowing her friend. "I'd almost forgotten."

"What's it for?" Cyndi whispered back as the three made their way toward the stage. "If it's another beauty-queen thing, I'll scream."

Jennifer lifted her shoulders. "Not my committee. Go up there and find out."

Cyndi did and was stunned to learn she'd been voted Most Successful. She accepted with tears in her eyes. Meredith also received an award—Best Disappearing Act. Cyndi and Jennifer exchanged glances at the tackiness of it, but Meredith accepted with a smile, telling her former classmates, "That's about to change."

And finally, just as Jennifer was glancing at her watch for the fortieth time and thinking about sneaking out to find Ryder, Meredith leaned over and whispered, "This is you."

"What?"

Meredith pointed to the stage and Jennifer looked up, surprised.

"...this person has given more to our class than any other. Even back in high school, a cheerleader and one of the most popular girls in school, she had time and a smile for everyone.

"She continued giving even after graduation. She headed up both our fifth-year reunion committee and this one. She's done our annual class newsletter every year for the past ten. She's given to numerous civic organizations, even taking time to coach Little League.

"This award is for everyone's friend, the sweetheart of the Hazelhurst High class of nineteen eighty-one...Jennifer Joyce!"

The ballroom broke out in applause. Cyndi and Meredith nudged her, urging her to rise. Still she sat, rooted to her seat, her stomach tied into a dozen different knots. Finally, hands shaking, she stood and started for the stage.

There, she accepted both the award and the congratulatory kiss from a former classmate, then turned and gazed out at the audience.

She cleared her throat. "You've caught me by surprise with this...and I don't quite know what to say." She found the faces of her two old friends. They both smiled and nodded their encouragement, and she cleared her throat again. "No, that's not true, I do know what to say. I want to tell you a story."

Jennifer thought of Ryder and squared her shoulders. "Once upon a time there was a boy from the wrong side of the tracks and a girl from the right side. He supported and believed in her, but when her friendship, her belief in him, was tested, she turned her back on him."

Jennifer lowered her eyes to the plaque in her hands, then looked out at her former classmates once more. "The people of this town—and this class—also treated him badly. He was judged by circumstantial evidence, was judged not by who he was but where he came from."

Her eyes filled, but she didn't try to blink them away, didn't try to steel herself from her emotions or from letting them show. "Being a friend is about trusting and sharing and supporting. It's about believing wholeheartedly even when popular opinion or evidence suggests otherwise.

"Those of you who still live here know by now what's been happening at the plant, of Lansing's intention to close it down and of the ramifications of such a thing happening.

"This boy, now a man, came back to town and proved himself a real friend. He could have sought revenge—indeed he had our fates in the palm of his hand—and who could have really blamed him? But instead he chose to help us, and because of him Hazelhurst has another chance."

Her fingers shook so badly Jennifer feared she might drop the award, and she tightened them on it. When she spoke again, tears choked her voice. "This man showed me I'm not the person I wanted to be...that I hadn't been for a very long time. He showed me what a real friend was and how wrong I'd been about so many things in the past."

She circled her gaze over the ballroom, stopping on a lone figure at the edge of the crowd. Ryder stood there, his back against the doors that led into the garden. He wore his leather jacket and jeans instead of evening clothes; his expression gave nothing away.

Jennifer's heartbeat slowed, her chest swelled with love. She took the deepest, steadiest breath she had in years and shifted her gaze back at her former classmates.

"Once upon a time," she finished, her voice strong and clear, "I asked how I would explain him and me. Now I know... I'd tell everyone and anyone that I love him."

The tears came then, filling her eyes, threatening to overflow. "I don't deserve this award, but I know someone who does. Excuse me."

The ballroom was absolutely quiet as she started down the stage. Then she heard lone clapping, and she knew where it originated—Cyndi and Meredith. Her friends.

The clapping caught on until the room rang with it. It took her several minutes to get to the edge of the ballroom, winding her way through tables, being waylaid by well-wishers.

When she finally reached the spot where she'd seen Ryder, he was gone.

Her stomach crashed to her toes, and Jennifer looked around wildly. She had to find him, had to make him believe her! Panicked, she started for the main doors that would lead to the lobby and parking lot, then stopped and turned back to the glass doors and the garden beyond.

If he meant for her to find him, he had gone into the garden.

Crossing her fingers, she slipped through the doors. She followed the same path she and he had the night of the prom, around the pool and to the very center of the garden.

He was there. He was waiting for her.

The relief that flowed through her was the sweetest she'd ever known. She crossed to him, stopping close enough to touch but not touching. She clasped her hands together, and for long moments they stared at each other.

Finally, almost under his breath, Ryder murmured, "In there, you didn't have to do that."

"Yes... I did." She drew a deep breath. "I wanted everyone to know what kind of man you are, and I wanted them to know how much I love you."

Ryder gazed at her expression, realizing something about her had changed—there was a determination to the way she held herself, a ferocity in her eyes he'd never seen before. He used to dream that someday she'd look at him with that exact expression... the same expression he knew she could read in his eyes right now.

He opened his mouth, anxious to tell her why he'd come tonight, but she placed her fingers lightly against his lips.

"I'm sorry, Ryder—sorry I hurt you, sorry I didn't believe in you." Emotion choked the words, and she swallowed. "But most of all, I'm sorry I didn't see just how much you meant to me."

Jennifer dropped her hands to his chest. "You were my everything back then," she said softly. "But I was too young and silly to see it. Too scared of what I felt for you to acknowledge it. But now I not only see it, I know it with every fiber of my being."

The leather of his jacket was cool against her palms, and she slipped her hands underneath to the warmth of his chest. His heart beat almost wildly under her fingers. "You could have died on that motorcycle, Ryder. You almost did. It terrified me that I'd almost lost you. In that split second before I learned all of what had happened, when I'd thought it was you who'd . . . I almost died myself."

She drew a deep, shuddering breath. "When I came to see you at the hospital, I was furious at you for breaking your promise about the bike, devastated over Sonny's lie and over your abandoning me the night before. And Sonny was dead. I said awful things to you, things you didn't deserve, things I didn't mean. But at that moment blaming you was less painful than acknowledging all the things I really felt, including guilt."

The tears spilled over, and Jennifer didn't bother to wipe them away. "Then I did lose you. You left me, too. Without saying goodbye."

"Ah, Jen . . ." He cupped her face in his palms, brushing at the tears with his thumbs. "There's so much I have to tell you, so much I—"

"No, Ryder." Mirroring him, she cupped his face in her hands. "Let me finish now, before I lose the words to emotion."

She whispered her fingers over his face, reveling in the texture of his skin, in the hard planes of his jaw and chin. "The night of the prom I turned Sonny away, even though he professed to love me, because I ached from the things you'd said, because I saw the truth in them. I turned Sonny away because it was you I wanted . . . you I loved."

She trailed her thumbs across his lips; they trembled under her touch, and hope ballooned inside her. "I made Sonny into a hero, when I had a real hero all along." She dropped her hands to his shoulders. "Tell me it's not too late, Ryder. Tell me I haven't lost you for good."

He tangled his fingers in her hair, savoring the sensation he'd almost condemned himself to a lifetime without. "How could you have lost me when you're half of what I am? I said I didn't believe in you—that was a lie. I said I couldn't escape loving you— I didn't want to try. I said those things and held myself from you because I was afraid of being hurt. And when you offered the out, I jumped at it."

He brushed his mouth against hers. "Self-preservation runs strong in a kid from the wrong side of town."

"God, I love you." Jennifer leaned against him, pressing her face into his shoulder. She breathed in his scent—of leather and soap and riding against the wind.

Ryder held her to him, feeling whole and hopeful for the first time since the night he'd come to her window all those years ago. He smiled and pressed his lips to her hair. "We've gone all around the truth, Jen. We tried denying the past, we've wished we could change it . . . we've let it control us."

"And now?" she asked, tipping her face back up to his, her voice a husky whisper.

He moved his hands through her hair once more, the strands feathering through and around his fingers. "Now we have to accept it and go on. We have to accept the fact that sometimes the past, and its pain, will come back to haunt us. And when it does, we'll feel uncertain or vulnerable or afraid. But without the past there would be no you and me. It's part of who

we are. It happened as it did because of the fire between us.''

He caught her mouth in a brief but shattering kiss.
When he lifted his head, his expression was almost
fierce.

''We've been Ryder and Jennifer all along . . . that's
the point. We can't be anything else. And I don't want
to be anything else.''

She laughed then, giddy and dizzy and drunk with
happiness. ''What made you realize the truth?''

''Missing you so damn bad.''

She laughed again and hugged him. ''Let's go
home.''

They took the bike, leaving her car behind to be
picked up later. Jennifer wrapped her arms around his
middle and, pressing her chest to his back, held him as
tightly as she could, vowing to never let him go again.
And when they got to her house, they climbed the
stairs and made love in her big, soft bed.

Afterward, as they lay cuddling together, whispering words of love and fulfillment, Jennifer thought
again of her old friends. She smiled to herself, anticipating sharing her happiness with them.

She tipped her head back and met Ryder's sleepy,
satisfied gaze. ''I met with Cyndi and Meredith today.''

He brushed the damp tendrils of hair away from her
face. ''How'd it go?''

''Wonderfully. An old wound has begun to heal—
for all of us. We're going to keep in touch this time—
stay friends.'' She lowered her eyes and voice. ''Seeing them helped me realize I couldn't let you go so

easily. I decided then that I'd do whatever necessary to win you back.''

He pressed his mouth against hers in a long, breath-stealing kiss.

''What was that for?'' she asked as he lifted his head.

''Anything,'' he said simply. ''Everything.''

She drew his head to hers, mimicking him, stealing his breath this time. She smiled against his mouth. ''Ditto.''

For long moments they let the silence surround them, comfortable with it and each other.

After a while, Ryder propped himself on an elbow and looked down at her. ''The meeting this morning went well.''

''I was there.''

''You came?''

He lifted his eyebrows in surprise, and she saw the pleasure in his eyes. ''It killed me to see you. But yes, I came.'' She rubbed her cheek along his shoulder. ''I left before you said your part— I'm not that much of a masochist. Did the employees lose any of their enthusiasm?''

''It's a big step, and when I gave them all the figures they sobered a bit. But they voted—unanimously—to go forward anyway.''

''What's next?''

''Financing. There are a lot of variables that need to fit together for us to pull this thing off, but I'm optimistic.''

Jennifer cuddled against him, looking up at him through her lashes. ''And what about the future?''

Ryder arched one dark, sweeping brow. "The future?"

"You know...us...like in Mr. and Mrs. Together Forever."

He grinned. "Is that a proposal, Ms. Joyce?"

"It is," she said, meeting his gaze squarely, all business now. "What's your answer?"

"Can I have some time to think it over?"

"Absolutely not. You've had ten years already."

He laughed, pushing her onto her back and pinning her there. "I accept, then."

"We're engaged?" she murmured breathlessly.

"I guess so."

"What should I tell Susan?"

"Susan?"

"My business partner." Jennifer made a sound of frustration. "When will we be leaving?"

"Would you like to stay?"

"Would you?"

"Yes." At her expression—at once perplexed and delighted—he laughed. "I'm as surprised as you. But Hazelhurst has grown on me. And, your father seems to think, if all goes down the way we hope, that he and I might make a pretty good team."

"Oh, Ryder..."

Happy beyond words, Jennifer brought her mouth to his.

* * * * *

Silhouette Special Edition

COMING NEXT MONTH

#697 NAVY BABY—Debbie Macomber
Hard-living sailor Riley never thought he'd settle down with a
preacher's daughter. But he couldn't steer clear of Hannah and their
navy baby, though it meant riding out the storm of his life.

#698 SLOW LARKIN'S REVENGE—Christine Rimmer
Local bad boy Winslow Larkin, was back in town . . . and out to
seduce the one woman who'd almost tamed his heart years ago. But
loving Violet Windemere proved much sweeter than revenge!

#699 TOP OF THE MOUNTAIN—Mary Curtis
The memory of Lili Jamison's high school passion lived on in her love
child. Reuniting with Brad Hollingsworth rekindled the actual
fire . . . and the guilt of her eleven-year-old secret.

#700 ROMANCING RACHEL—Natalie Bishop
Rachel Stone had her hands full raising her stepson on her own.
When strong, stern Tyrrell Rafferty III entered the picture, he
completed the family portrait . . . better than she knew!

#701 THE MAN SHE MARRIED—Tracy Sinclair
Teenager Dorian Merrill had fled her hometown and broken marriage
to find her fortune. Now the *woman* was back, a penthouse success—
but lured to the other side of town by the man she married.

#702 CHILD OF THE STORM—Diana Whitney
When Megan O'Connor lost her beloved sister, she vowed not to lose
her seven-year-old nephew. Not even to his father, who resurfaced to
claim him . . . and Megan's heart.

AVAILABLE THIS MONTH:

#691 OBSESSION
Lisa Jackson

#692 FAMILY FRIENDLY
Jo Ann Algermissen

#693 THE HEALING TOUCH
Christine Flynn

#694 A REAL CHARMER
Jennifer Mikels

#695 ANNIE IN THE MORNING
Curtiss Ann Matlock

#696 LONGER THAN . . .
Erica Spindler

Silhouette Special Edition

presents

SONNY'S GIRLS

by Emilie Richards, Celeste Hamilton and Erica Spindler

They had been Sonny's girls, irresistibly drawn to the charismatic high school football hero. Ten years later, none could forget the night that changed their lives forever.

In July—
ALL THOSE YEARS AGO by Emilie Richards (SSE #684)
Meredith Robbins had left town in shame. Could she ever banish the past and reach for love again?

In August—
DON'T LOOK BACK by Celeste Hamilton (SSE #690)
Cyndi Saint was Sonny's steady. Ten years later, she remembered only his hurtful parting words....

In September—
LONGER THAN . . . by Erica Spindler (SSE #696)
Bubbly Jennifer Joyce was everybody's friend. But nobody knew the secret longings she felt for bad boy Ryder Hayes....

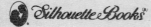

SILHOUETTE®
OFFICIAL SWEEPSTAKES
RULES

NO PURCHASE NECESSARY

1. To enter, complete an Official Entry Form or 3" × 5" index card by hand-printing, in plain block letters, your complete name, address, phone number and age, and mailing it to: Silhouette Fashion A Whole New You Sweepstakes, P.O. Box 9056, Buffalo, NY 14269-9056.

   No responsibility is assumed for lost, late or misdirected mail. Entries must be sent separately with first class postage affixed, and be received no later than December 31, 1991 for eligibility.

2. Winners will be selected by D.L. Blair, Inc., an independent judging organization whose decisions are final, in random drawings to be held on January 30, 1992 in Blair, NE at 10:00 a.m. from among all eligible entries received.

3. The prizes to be awarded and their approximate retail values are as follows: Grand Prize — A brand-new Ford Explorer 4×4 plus a trip for two (2) to Hawaii, including round-trip air transportation, six (6) nights hotel accommodation, a $1,400 meal/spending money stipend and $2,000 cash toward a new fashion wardrobe (approximate value: $28,000) or $15,000 cash; two (2) Second Prizes — A trip to Hawaii, including round-trip air transportation, six (6) nights hotel accommodation, a $1,400 meal/spending money stipend and $2,000 cash toward a new fashion wardrobe (approximate value: $11,000) or $5,000 cash; three (3) Third Prizes — $2,000 cash toward a new fashion wardrobe. All prizes are valued in U.S. currency. Travel award air transportation is from the commercial airport nearest winner's home. Travel is subject to space and accommodation availability, and must be completed by June 30, 1993. Sweepstakes offer is open to residents of the U.S. and Canada who are 21 years of age or older as of December 31, 1991, except residents of Puerto Rico, employees and immediate family members of Torstar Corp., its affiliates, subsidiaries, and all agencies, entities and persons connected with the use, marketing, or conduct of this sweepstakes. All federal, state, provincial, municipal and local laws apply. Offer void wherever prohibited by law. Taxes and/or duties, applicable registration and licensing fees, are the sole responsibility of the winners. Any litigation within the province of Quebec respecting the conduct and awarding of a prize may be submitted to the Régie des loteries et courses du Québec. All prizes will be awarded; winners will be notified by mail. No substitution of prizes is permitted.

4. Potential winners must sign and return any required Affidavit of Eligibility/Release of Liability within 30 days of notification. In the event of noncompliance within this time period, the prize may be awarded to an alternate winner. Any prize or prize notification returned as undeliverable may result in the awarding of that prize to an alternate winner. By acceptance of their prize, winners consent to use of their names, photographs or their likenesses for purposes of advertising, trade and promotion on behalf of Torstar Corp. without further compensation. Canadian winners must correctly answer a time-limited arithmetical question in order to be awarded a prize.

5. For a list of winners (available after 3/31/92), send a separate stamped, self-addressed envelope to: Silhouette Fashion A Whole New You Sweepstakes, P.O. Box 4665, Blair, NE 68009.

PREMIUM OFFER TERMS

To receive your gift, complete the Offer Certificate according to directions. Be certain to enclose the required number of "Fashion A Whole New You" proofs of product purchase (which are found on the last page of every specially marked "Fashion A Whole New You" Silhouette or Harlequin romance novel). Requests must be received no later than December 31, 1991. Limit: four (4) gifts per name, family, group, organization or address. Items depicted are for illustrative purposes only and may not be exactly as shown. Please allow 6 to 8 weeks for receipt of order. Offer good while quantities of gifts last. In the event an ordered gift is no longer available, you will receive a free, previously unpublished Silhouette or Harlequin book for every proof of purchase you have submitted with your request, plus a refund of the postage and handling charge you have included. Offer good in the U.S. and Canada only.

SLFW - SWPR

SILHOUETTE® OFFICIAL SWEEPSTAKES ENTRY FORM

4-FWSES-2

Complete and return this Entry Form immediately – the more entries you submit, the better your chances of winning!

- Entries must be received by **December 31, 1991.**
- A Random draw will take place on **January 30, 1992.**
- No purchase necessary.

Yes, I want to win a FASHION A WHOLE NEW YOU Sensuous and Adventurous prize from Silhouette:

Name _____ Telephone _____ Age _____

Address _____

City _____ State _____ Zip _____

Return Entries to: Silhouette **FASHION A WHOLE NEW YOU,**
P.O. Box 9056, Buffalo, NY 14269-9056   © 1991 Harlequin Enterprises Limited

PREMIUM OFFER

To receive your free gift, send us the required number of proofs-of-purchase from any specially marked FASHION A WHOLE NEW YOU Silhouette or Harlequin Book with the Offer Certificate properly completed, plus a check or money order (do not send cash) to cover postage and handling payable to Silhouette FASHION A WHOLE NEW YOU Offer. We will send you the specified gift.

OFFER CERTIFICATE

Item	A. SENSUAL DESIGNER VANITY BOX COLLECTION (set of 4) (Suggested Retail Price $60.00)	B. ADVENTUROUS TRAVEL COSMETIC CASE SET (set of 3) (Suggested Retail Price $25.00)
# of proofs-of-purchase	18	12
Postage and Handling	$3.50	$2.95
Check one	☐	☐

Name _____

Address _____

City _____ State _____ Zip _____

Mail this certificate, designated number of proofs-of-purchase and check or money order for postage and handling to: Silhouette **FASHION A WHOLE NEW YOU Gift Offer,** P.O. Box 9057, Buffalo, NY 14269-9057. Requests must be received by December 31, 1991.

ONE PROOF-OF-PURCHASE

4-FWSEP-2

To collect your fabulous free gift you must include the necessary number of proofs-of-purchase with a properly completed Offer Certificate.

© 1991 Harlequin Enterprises Limited

See previous page for details.